THE INDIAN CASTE SYSTEM, THE OPPRESSION OF DALITS AND SOME WAYS TO END THEM

Rathnam Indurthy, Ph. D

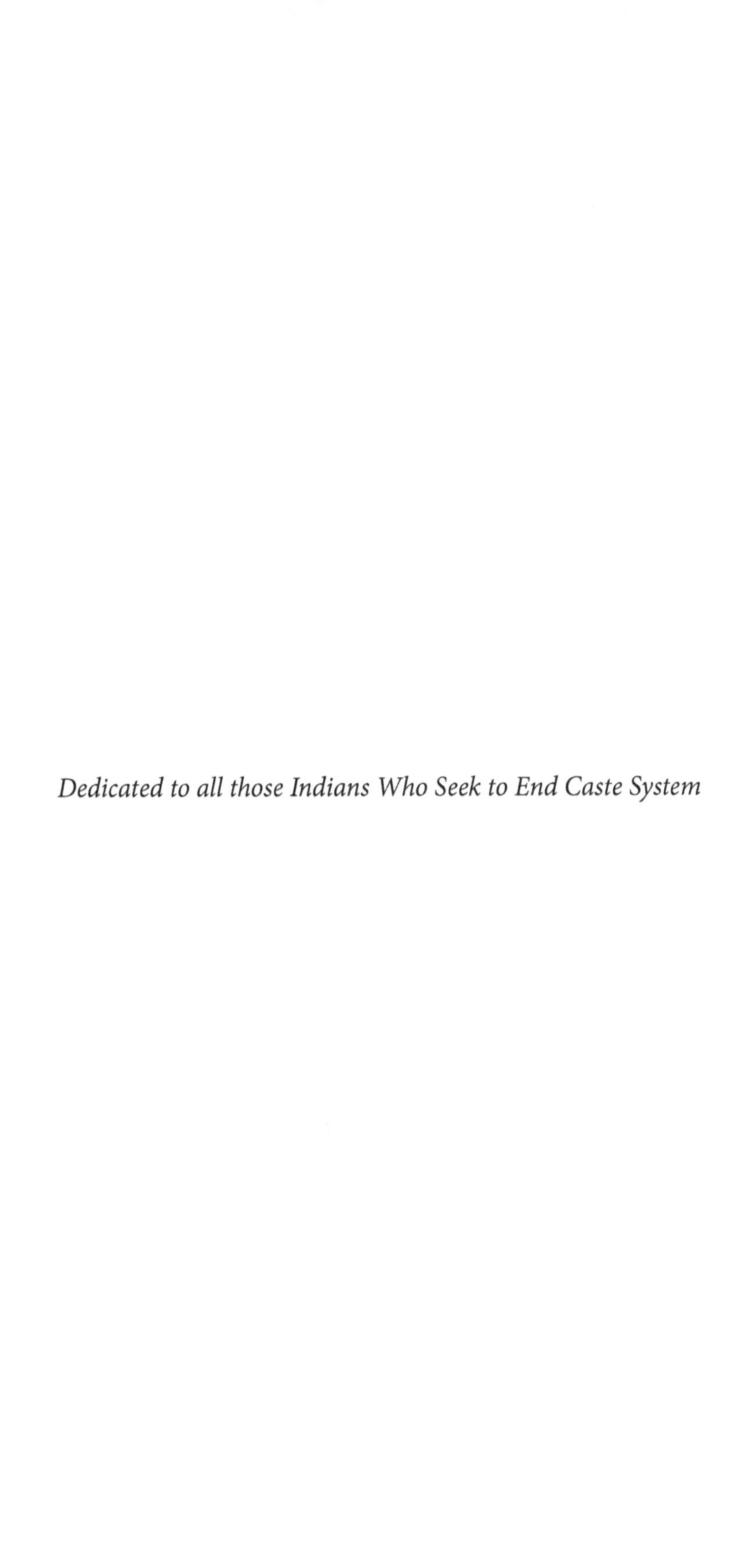

Dedicated to all those Indians Who Seek to End Caste System

Contents

Preface

India, perhaps, is unique in its centuries-old rigid, persistent hierarchical caste system. Initially, under the Rigveda of about 2,000 BC, Indian society was divided into four classes of people: Brahmans (priests), Kshatriyas (warriors), Vaisyas (merchants), and Sudras (labourers) but providing for social mobility from one class to another based one's skills and merit. However, during the Manu Shastra period, such as under the Manu Smriti (250 BC- 250 AD), this social mobility came to an end. The Manu Smriti created a rigid hierarchical system, calling the first three classes of people "pure" and the Sudras "impure" based on their birth and occupation of karma, prescribing their respective duties and obligations. It (or its author, Manu) created another class of people known as Chandalas (untouchables) outside the caste hierarchy, obligating them to do the most dehumanising tasks in service of other groups. Muslim invaders and, thereafter, rulers who ruled India for more than 900 years from the 9th century to the 18th century basically did not disturb the caste system except that some of them had dismantled temples and committed a forced conversion of Hindus to Islam. The British, who had succeeded the Muslim empire, ruled India for 250 years, including the East India Company, did not do much either to the caste system other than listing the former untouchables as Scheduled castes (SC) and /or scheduled tribes (ST) primarily for the purpose of census and grant them some representation in provincial legislative council beginning in the 1930s as a separate bloc. It was only after India's independence in 1947, under its Constitution of 1950, that untouchability, at least on paper, was outlawed, and the former untouchables (Dalits) were granted representation both in central and state legislatures and as well as reservations in the areas of education and jobs through on temporary basis to end their naked discrimination and oppression from caste Hindus and improve their socio-economic conditions. Although the Dalits have made some tangible progress, the bulk of them, especially those who live in rural areas, continue to suffer isolation, segregation, discrimination, and oppression from caste Hindus, including lynchings and atrocities, and they have increased under the Modi Government (1014-Present). So, our purpose is, first, examine the origins of the caste system its theories, features and functions and the foreign rulers- both Muslim and the British had handled the caste system in India; second, describe the socio-economic and educational conditions are awful and pitiful and why they continue to live in object poverty, and continue to face discrimination and oppression from the case Hindus; third, identify beliefs and practices of major religions such as Christianity, Islam and Buddhism an, their views of men, women and slavery and their distortions and their role in India; fourth, we present certain ways or measures on how to root out the caste system and ultimately the Dalit discrimination and oppression, and finally in we conclusion con and in summation we reflect India can become an egalitarian exemplary democracy by choosing secular leaders who have a broad vision and who are dedicated and committed to serving for the common good of all men and women in India, regardless of their caste, creed, ethnicity and religion.

Introduction

The caste system originated with the arrival of Aryans and their founding of Vedas and other sacred scriptures around the second century BC. As noted in the preface, the *purusha Shakta of* Rigveda of 2,000 BC divides Indian society into four-fold (chaturvarnya*)* varnas (divisions or races), which comprise several castes (Jatis). The supreme creator, Brahma, gave birth to Brahmans (priests) from his mouth, the Kshatriyas (warriors) from his shoulders, the Vaishyas from his thighs and Sudras (labourers) from his feet. Manu, the law-giver, in his Manu Smriti (250 BC-@50 AD) reaffirms this four-fold division scheme, prescribing the tasks of each group, besides creating an additional group of people outside the caste hierarchy (Avranas) whom he calls Chandalas (untouchables), the polluting class of people relegating them to do menial tasks such cremating dead bodies, cleaning human bodily fluids, skinning and removing dead animals. Manu affirmed the caste system as rigid, based on birth and hereditary on account of karma. Today, they are called Dalits beginning in the 1930s and account for about 18% percent of India's population. As we have already noted in the preface, The purpose of this work is, first, to preset the theories of the caste system for its continuation; second, to present a brief discussion of how other major religions view men, women and slavery; third, examine briefly the current conditions of Dalits in India and why they have gotten worse under Modi Government and identify the kinds of atrocities being perpetrated by caste Hindus against them, and finally, present a few suggestions on how to end both this baneful caste system and the Dalit oppression I=in India.

CHAPTER – 1

The Caste System: Its Theories, History, its Features and Functions

There are various theories or perspectives that explain the persistence of the caste system in India. In 2019, Mr Rehna R. Rehna produced an excellent booklet for IAS exams in which he presents five theories of the caste system, its features, and its functions and dysfunctions. We want to cite and discuss them briefly here below:

Traditional or Ideological Theory.

This theory is based on *religious* texts such *as Rigveda and the Manu Smriti.* For example, *the Manu* code considers the Brahmans, Kshatriyas, and Vaishyas as twice-born and pure, while Sudras are once-born and "impure." Women, if they are born into the pure category, consider them impure along with the Sudras and treat the untouchables as chattel. It is considered the most important theory. We cite some examples of this theory views Sudras, women, and untouchables:

Shudras:

1. The Shudras are created to serve the upper varnas to serve faithfully with devotion without grumbling and they are born of mating between Brahmans and Sudras.

2. The Brahmans should never invite persons of other varnas for food.

3. He who instructs Shudra pupils and whose teacher is a Shudra shall become disqualified from being invited to a Shradha.

4. A Shudra is unfit to receive education.

5. Let him (Brahman) not live in a country where rulers are Shudras.

6. He must never read Vedas in the presence of Shudras.

7. A Shubra who insults a twice-born man with gross invectives shall have his tongue cut out as he is of low origin.

8. If a Shudra arrogantly presumes to preach religion to Brahmans, the king shall have poured burning oil on his mouth and ears.

9. A Brahman may compel a Shudra, whether bought or unbought, to do servile work, for he is created to be a slave of Brahman.

10. No Shudra will have no property of his own.

11. A Shudra who wants to just fill his stomach may serve a Vaishya.

12. The most sacred duty of Shudra is to serve the Brahmans, always reciting the words" Brahman "with utmost devotion" and many other obligations in service of the twice-born[1].

Women.

Regardless of their birth in the upper varna, women remain impure like the Shudras. We cite examples of how they are viewed by the Manu Smriti.

1. Day and night, women must be kept dependent by the males, and if they attach themselves to sensual enjoyment, they must be kept under one's control.

2. Her father protects (her)in childhood, her husband protects (her) in youth, and her sons protect (her) in old age. A woman is never fit for independence.

3. The highest duty of all castes, even weak husbands, strive to protect their wives.

4. Let (Husband) employ his (wife) in the collection and expenditure of his wealth, in keeping (everything) clean in religious duties, in preparation of his food, and in looking after household utensils.

---

[1] **Chapter 1: The Theories of Caste System**
"Vastiest verses from Manusmriti-law Book of Hindus," *Velivada* May 31, 2017 athttps://velivada.com/2017/05/31/castiest-quotes-verses-manusmriti-law-book-hindus/,

5. Women do not care for beauty, nor are their attention fixed on age; they are men, and they give themselves to the handsome and to the ugly.

6. Through their passion for men, through their mutable temper, and through their natural heartlessness, they become disloyal towards their husbands. However, they may be carefully guarded.

7. Manu allotted women beds, seats, and ornaments, impure desires, wrath, dishonesty, malice, and bad conduct.

8. For women, no rite with sacred books; thus, the law is settled; women are destitute of strength and destitute of Vedic texts, falsehood, that is a fixed rule[2].

Untouchables (Dalits).

Untouchables (Dalits) are put outside the caste hierarchy and are classified as Chandalas and polluting, according to the Manu Smriti.

1. Chandalas must live outside the village, use discarded vessels, and wear the clothes of the dead, as well as ornaments of iron.

2. They could not walk about villages and cities at night.

3. They had to dispose of those of the dead bodies. Of those who had no relatives and served as executioners.

4. As scavengers, they were required to live outside the city[3].

Racial Theory

The Sanskrit word for varna means colour, and the classification of the Brahmans (priests), Kshatriyas (warriors) and Vaishyas (merchants) and Shudras (domestic servants). The Vedic texts identifies differences between Aryans and non-Aryans (Dasa-Shudras) not only in their complexion but

---

[2] At https://hindutvawatch.org/manusmriti-law-for-dalits-and-women.
[3] At https://www.starhaks.com/2820590/duties-mentioned-manusmriti—concerning-chandalas—outside-village—discarded—untensels.

also in their speech, religious practice, and physical features, perhaps the Dravidians. The varna system was based on birth and occupation.

Political Theory

This theory is based on the premise that it was the clever instrument invented by Brahmins to place themselves on the highest of the social hierarcto to dominate the rest of the Indian society.

Occupational theory

As caste hierarchy is based on one's occupation and hereditariness, the persons who are regarded as better and respectable, their professions are deemed superior to those than those who engage in dirty professions. As such occupational differences has divided the Indian society into higher castes and lower castes and subcastes of people.

Evolution Theory

According to this theory, the caste system has not come into existence suddenly; rather, it is the result of a long process of social evolution. The factors which may have influenced this process are as follows:

1. Hereditary occupations.

2. The Brahams desire to themselves to be pure.

3. The lack of rigid unitary control of the state.

4. The unwillingness of rulers to enforce a uniform standard of law and custom.

5. The karma and Dharma doctrines also explain for the origin and continuation of caste system: Karma determines ones birth as a result of one's deeds done in his/her previous life, and if one lives according his caste, he is living by Dharma.

6. Ideas of exclusive family, ancestor worship, and clash of the sacramental work.

7. Clash of antagonistic cultures, particularly patriarchal and matriarchal systems.

8. Clash of races, colour prejudices and conquest.

9. Deliberate economic and administrative policies adopted by various conquerors.

10. The geographical isolation of the Indian peninsula, and

11. Foreign invasions[4].

Although some of the theories may explain the caste system, the Vedic texts, especially the Manu Smriti texts, have an enduring and delible impact on caste and its persistent continuation. For these are sacred and divinely inspired texts obligating Indians to follow their injunctions with unquestioned devotion and commitment. As quoted above, Manu Smriti puts three castes-

Brahmans, Kshatriyas and Vaishyas are at the top as pure and degrade Shudra women and dehumanise the untouchables. Sanskar Bharti notes Manu Smriti is a set of rules for society reiterating a watertight, hierarchical caste structure. It is believed to be the fountainhead of *varnashrama dharma*, the four stages of human life a devote Hindu is told to strive for. " Bharti quotes noted historian Harbans Muhira, who said, "it is one of the fundamental texts of the Brahminical order of Hindu society. Even as Hindu society, like others, has seldom totally conformed to any overarching vision and even as it has been evolving over centuries"[5]. Mr. P. B. Sawant, former Supreme Court Judge, contends that before the Aryans had arrived in India, India was "more advanced, urbanised, peaceful and relatively prosperous" as depicted by the Indus civilisation. He argues that the Aryans who came from the Caucasus region have divided India by writing books such as the Manu Smriti, which placed the Brahmans at the top of the societal ladder of the four-fold division and castes. Sawant blames the Aryans for creating a social order to ensure that they would always be at the top and own all the wealth and power by dividing the people into four hierarchical groups,

---

[4] Reha R. Rehna, "caste System in India: Origins, Features, and Functions," *Clear IAS*, March9, 2019, at htps://www.clearias.com/caste-system-in-india.

[5] Sanskar Bharti, "Manusmriti in Modi Era," *Frontline*, at https://frontline.thehindu.com/social-issues-mansmriti-in-modi-era/article2359595.ece

what is known as castes, assigning each their duties and obligations based on birth by putting Brahmans at the top and other groups in descending order of status and privilege. These duties and obligations "were fixed for life. watertight, and immutable. Marriages between them were not permitted, nor would they eat together." As an example, the Manu Smriti, Sawant notes, obligates the Shudras to serve the other three superior castes; it denied education to them and women and prohibited foreign travel to keep people in isolation. He accuses the Aryans of using the device of divide and rule by creating a caste system based on prejudice and dividing Indian society into various social groups with conflicting interests and antagonisms towards each other[6]. Jainism and Buddhism came about as a reaction to the Caste system in the 6th century, But as a large number of Hindus began to embrace Buddhism, the revival of Hinduism launched by Adi Sankara Charya in the 9th century neutralised the spreading of Buddhism. Dr B.R Ambedkar was so disgusted with Manu Smriti's degrading treatment of untouchables in December 1927 that he burnt its copies in a bonfire, and in October 1956, he rejected Hinduism and embraced Buddhis along with more than 3000,000 of his followers. Dr Ambedkar, the architect of India's Constitution who provided affirmative action programmes for the Dalits in it, denounced the RSS for its espousal of Hindutva doctrine as anti-national, divisive, and destructive to India's unity and integrity. Here below, we want to look at briefly how the foreign Muslim rulers who had ruled India for more than 900 years from the 8th century to the 16th century and the British rulers who ruled it for more than 150 years had dealt with the Indian caste system and their impact on India. We also want to examine how Independent India has been in dealing with the caste system and its ramifications since its independence in 1947.

The Muslim Rule and its Impact (1,000-1757):

Muslim invaders had invaded India from central Asia, Persia (Iran) and Afghanistan since the 8th century and had established their empires under different dynasties. Matthew McClinton, who had reviewed the literature on Muslim rule, notes that the Hindu stratified system was not affected much

---

[6] B.B. Sawant, "The Manusmriti and a Divided nation," *The Wire*, November 16, 2020, at https://thewire.in/caste/manusmriti-history-discrimination—constitution.

by the introduction of Islam and that not many Hindus had converted to Islam, though it is a monotheistic religion[7]. However, Akhlesh Pillalmargi points out the Muslim ruler had destroyed many Hindu temples and urban centres to assert their power in India. He notes Mohammad Ghor had sacked the Somanath temple in the Western part of India in 1025, and it was destroyed by Alauddin Khilji in Delhi in 1299; another incarnation of the temple was destroyed by the Mughal emperor Aurangzeb; in 1528, a mosque was built what was allegedly once a temple at the birthplace of God Rama. He had destroyed many Hindu temples, including the famous Vishwanath temple[8]. Judge Sawant notes during the Mughal empire, in the latter half of the 16th century, Islam became a way out for depressed people such as the Shudras who had converted to it. A few upper classes, too, had converted to Islam for material and other benefits. He adds that contrary to current propaganda, not more than 5% of the land was forcible converts[9]. As Dr Ejaz notes, 75% percent of Muslims in India are from the Dalit classes who have converted to escape oppression from caste Hindus and out of conviction[10]. Kancha Iliaiah and Mohsina Ansari write the current BJP Government under Modi falsely accuses Muslim rulers that they had introduced untouchability in India. The authors seek to clear the myth that Islam came to India through Muslim invaders like Muhammad bin Qasim, who invaded India in 715. They point out that Islam came to India with a Kerala Sudra king, Cheramaan Permal, who went to Mecca on his own, met the Prophet Mohammad around 622, embraced Islam, and spread it in Kerala and other parts of South India[11].

---

[7] Matthew McClinton, "Jati: A History of Caste Systemin Ancient, Medieval and Modern India" Brewminate, September 9, 2023, at https://brewminate.com/jati—a-history-of-the-caste-system -in-ancient-medieval-and-modern-india

[8] Akhilesh Pillalamarri, "India's Right is Correct About One thing: India's Muslim Rulers did Destroy Hindu Temples," *The Diplomat,*August 3, 2016, at https://thediplomat.com/2016/08/indias-hindu-right—is-one-one-thing-indias-muslim-rulers-did-destroy-hindu-temples/

[9] Sawant, "Manusmriti and a Divided Nation."

[10] "Dalit Muslims" *out looindia,* January, 27, 2022, at htpps://www.outlookindia.com/website/story//dalit-muslims/201644.

[11] Kancha Ilaiah and Mohasina Ansari, "Was untouchability in India Created by Islam?" *The Mill Gazette, April 11, 2016, at https://www.themillgazette./news/7-analysis/14116-was-untouchability-created-in-india-by-islam/*

The British Rule and its Impact (1757-1857, and 1858-1947):

The Britishers came to India as the East India Company in 1608 and took control of most of India in 1757 following the collapse of the Mughal empire. However, with the mutiny of Indians in 1857, India came under the direct control of the British Government, which ended in 1947. The British rulers had only reinforced the caste system, and in fact, it rigidified it, although they opened educational opportunities to Indians by establishing schools and colleges and permitted Christian missionaries who did magnificent work by starting schools, colleges, and hospitals for the poor especially Dalits who embraced Christian faith inspired by its emphasis on equality, fraternity, and oneness. Mr McClinton points out that by introducing a census beginning in 1881 and thereafter every ten years, the British colonial rulers used caste (Jati) and zoological classifications "aiming to establish who was superior to whom by virtue of their supposed purity, occupational origins and collective moral worth." The British officials. He notes, "the census-determined Jatis to decide which group of people were qualified for which jobs" in the Government and people of "which Jatis to be excluded as untouchables." McClinton thinks "the strict British class may have influenced the British colonial preoccupation with the caste system as well as with British perception of pre-colonial Indian castes. The British, coming from a society rigidly divided by class, attempted to equate India's castes with British social classes." McClinton adds that the British colonial Government also passed a series of laws based on religion and caste identities. For example, in 1871, the Criminal Tribes Act was enacted, declaring people belonging to certain castes as born with criminal tendencies. By the late 19th century, it included most Shudras and untouchables. It prepared a list of such castes and restricted the regions they could visit and the people they could socialise with. These laws were enforced until the mid-20th century, which created social divisions and different identities between and among Hindus. As social unrest erupted during the 1920s, laws prejudicial laws, the colonial Government adopted a positive discriminatory policy by reserving certain Government jobs for lower castes as scheduled casts and /or scheduled tribes. In 1932, upon request by Dr Ambedkar at the round table conference in London, Prime Minister of Britain Ramsay MacDonald awarded a provision for separate representation for Muslims, Sikhs, Christians and Dalits, which Mahatma Gandhi had opposed and following his fast unto death, Ambedkar withdrew his demand. This brief discussion indicates. How extensive and detrimental role did the British rulers play in perpetuating and reinforcing the caste system and its divisions rigidly and legally[12]?

The Hindu Reform Movements 19th-20th Century):

Recognising the ill- effects of the Cast caste system in the wake of British colonialism, several Indian leaders launched reform movements during the 19th -20th centuries to purge Hinduism of its negative aspects. We want to identify the names of a few leaders of these movements and what they stressed:

Raja Rammohan Roy Brahmo Samaj (1772-1833):

Raj Rammohan Roy founded the Brahma Samaj with the goal of purging Hinduism of its evil practices that crept into it over centuries. Roy believed in the doctrine of the unity of God like other monotheistic religions and opposed idol worship; he fiercely opposed the evil practice of Sati, widely prevalent at that time, and it was abolished by Governor General William Bentinck in 1829. Roy condemned polygamy and other forms of subjugation against women; Roy was an advocate of modern education and established an English school as well as a Vedanta college in 1825.

Keshab Chandra Sen (1838-84):

Keshab Chandra Sen joined the Brahma Samaj in 1858 and he took its activities beyond Calcutta into UP, Punjab, Chennai, and Mumbai.; he attacked caste system; promoted widow marriages; stressed universalism in religion.

Dayananda Saraswati and Arya Samaj (1824:

Arya Samaj was founded by Dayanand Saraswati from Gujrat. It was a revivalist movement, and it soon spread to many parts of India. In 1875' Saraswati wrote *Satyarth Prakash* to propagate the principles of Arya Samaj.

---

[12] McClinton, "JatiA History of Caste system in Ancient, medieval and Modern India."

Saraswati denounced the ritualistic aspects of Hindu religion and called for the preaching of Vedas; he attacked Puranas, polytheism, idolatry, and domination of the priestly class (Brahmans); opposed child marriages, and opposed a multiplicity of castes as he considered caste system as the primary cause of lower classes converting to Islam and Christianity.

Swami Vivekananda and Ramakrishna Mission (1863—1902):

Swami Vivekananda spread the message of spiritual Hinduism in the US and Europe during his tour of 1893-97. He established Ramakrishna Mission in 1897 and set up a Maa Math in Belur, Karnataka. He opposed a degeneration in religion, manifold divisions, caste rigidities, practice of untouchability and superstitions. Swami Vivekananda wanted Indians to learn work ethics, organisation skills and technological advances from the west.

Dr. Atmaram Pandurang (1823-98) and Prarthan Samaj:

Prarthana Samaj, an off shoot of Brahma Samj, a reform movement of Hinduism, was founded by Dr. Atmaram Pandurang, a physician in 1867 in Mumbai. The Prarthana Samaj denounced idolatry, priestly domination, caste rigidities, and advocated monotheism. It also advocated social reforms such as inter-dinning, intermarriages, widow remarriage, and uplift of women and depressed classes. Apart from Hindu sects, it drew inspiration from Christianity and Buddhism and sought truth in all religions.

Sri Narayan Guru (1886-1928) and Ezhava Movement:

Ezhava movement was a movement of untouchable Ezhava against Brahmin domination in Kerala started by Sri Narayan Guru himself an untouchable in the early 20th century. It rejected caste system and developed the concept of one caste, one religion and one God for mankind. But his disciple Ayappan made it into no caste, no religion, and no God for mankind.

E.V. Ramaswamy Naicker (1879-1974), and Self-Respect Movement:

Ramaswamy Naicker launched his self-respect movement in 1925 in Tamil Nadu with the goal of rejecting the Brahmanical religion, which he thought was exploiting the lower classes. This movement demanded more concessions and privileges to surpass that of Brahmans in education and social status; he advocated the right to lead a life with dignity and self-respect and do away with exploitative systems based on superstitions and beliefs; he called for the protection of women rights, the establishment of homes for orphan's widows and opening educational institutions for them. Ramaswamy attacked Manu Smriti, which he said had produced the caste system and founded Tamil journals to propagate his beliefs and demands[13]. These reform movements might have affected a small percentage of Hindus with respect to the caste system and Hindu religious beliefs and practices, but many of these ancient beliefs and practices, as stipulated by Manu Smriti, rigidly remain intact with most Indians. Let us look at how Independent India has dealt with the caste system in India.

Independent India and the Caste System (1947-Present):

Under the Indian Constitution promulgated in January 1950, under Articles 15 (4) and Article 16 (4), Independent India formalised the reservation for SCs and STS in central and state legislatures howler temporarily for ten years to lift up Dalits and Adivasis economically and socially as they suffered oppression for centuries under the caste system. This temporary clause has become almost permanent as the ten-year terms are repeated every ten years and again in 2020. The caste system was also abolished under the Constitution on paper. In 1951, with an amendment to Article 342, states were mandated to reserve seats for SCS and STs in educational institutions. To protect the Dalits from discrimination and violence, *the Protection of Civil Rights Act* was approved by the parliament to provide for the punishment for the offence of practising untouchability and other offences. During the 1970s, as the Dalits launched a movement opposing

---

13. This brief discussion of Hindu reform movements is drawn from "Hindu Reform Movement-Insights IAS" athttps://www.insightson.com/modern-indan-history/socio-religious—reform-movements-in-the-19th-20th-ce-india/hindu-reform-movements/

the use of the term Harijans, a term coined by Mahatma Gandhi in 1982, the Union Government asked all states not to use the word "harijan" for the SC's. But as reservations had fuelled retribution and violence against them by the upper-caste Hindus, it forced the parliament in 1989 to pass *Scheduled castes and Scheduled (Prevention of Atrocities Act)* to prevent atrocities such as assault, sexual exploitation, and denial of access to public places, as punishable under the law. In 1990, the union Government headed by Prime Minister V.P. Singh implemented the Mandal Commission's recommendations in 1990, allocating 27% of reservation for Other Backward Classes (OBC) even in the wake of protests by upper castes led by the BJP. These implementations dramatically changed India's socio-political landscape as they deepened the divide and tension between upper castes and Shudras. In 2017, the Supreme Court said the words Harijan and Dhobi are "offensive, insulting, and humiliating, are often used by the so-called upper-caste people for the members of Scheduled castes to keep them in a state of servitude." In 2018, the court said the Constitution had abolished un to untouchability, and therefore, the word "Harijan" should not be used. In 2018, the court asked the centre and states not to use the word "Dalit," which means oppressed or broken[14]. In 2020, proposed by the Modi Government of the Bhartiya Janata Party BJP), the 103rd amendment was approved, granting 10% reservation to economically weakened forward classes in jobs and in educational institutions. Over a period, both under Congress and non-congress-led governments, discrimination against Dalits had reduced, but beginning in 2014, under the Modi regime, discrimination, and atrocities, including lynchings, have increased largely. The RSS, which has mothered the BJP, believes in the caste system mandated by Manu Smriti, and it seeks to replace the Indian Constitution with its own along the lines of Manu Smriti. The ideological father and chief of the RSS/ Sangh Parivar M.S. Golwalkar (1940-70), defended the caste system stating that the social order stipulated by Manu Smriti was beneficial to India for the survival of Hindus and Hinduism with Brahmans sitting at the top of caste hierarchy as being selfless and endowed with knowledge to provide spiritual

---

[14] Darpan Singh, "Who is Dalit or Savam? Why Caste System must go In Totality," *India Today*, August 2022, at https://www.indiatoday.in/news-analysis/story/dalit-savam-caste-system-must-go-1989509-2022-08-18,and KBS Sidhu "Abolishing Caste System in India Sidh: Propositions and Perspectives" *medium*, March 2018, at https://kbssidhdu/abolishing-caste-system-in-india-prpositions-perspectivestbttb1fb5bae8b8 1961.medium.com

guidance to other castes.[15] As Sanskar Bharti points out, in his book "*We or Our Nationhood Defined*" Golwalkar proposed "the denial of the franchise to some sections of Indian society, that is minorities" India must return to the Golden age when a Dalit would be harshly punished if his passing shadow fell on a Brahma's body! And *mlechha* would remain way out of the sight of a pure Aryan, and women would produce lots of children[16]. The Dalis and Muslims are being assaulted, killed, and even lynched for their alleged killing and trading of cows- their sacred animal. Let us now identify the principal features of the caste system, as well as its functions and dysfunctions.

The Caste System's Features, Functions and Dysfunctions

Mr. Rehna presents the caste system's features, functions, and dysfunctions, which we want to cite in a condenseWd form:

The Principal Features:

1. **Division of Society**: The society is divided into castes in a pecking order from Brahmans to Shudras based on birth.

2. **Endogamy:** Members of castes and subcastes are required to marry in their own castes, failing which they will be ostracised and lose their castes.

3. **Hereditary Status and Occupation:** Hereditary occupation is imperative.

4. **Restriction on Food and Drink:** Upper castes, especially Brahmans, determine how food should be prepared, by whom, and by what kind of vessels. They are mandated not to eat food prepared by low castes. Eating beef is a taboo except for the Dalits.

5. **Name Particularity:** Usually, names are associated with a particular caste and even occupation.

---

[15] Aakar Patel, "Gowalkar's Hindutva worships Caste but pretends is inclusive and Above Caste" *National* earold, August 18, 2022, at https://www.nationalherold.com/national/goalkars-hindutva-worships-caste-but-pretends-it is inclusive-and-above-caste.

[16] Bharti, "Manusmriti in Modi Era."

6. **The Concept of Purity and Pollution:** Brahmans, Kshatriyas, and Vaishyas are ritually and racially pure, and as such, they are supposed to keep themselves away from Shudras, considered impure and polluting, and not touch them, especially the Dalits.

7. **Jati Panchayat:** Each caste is protected not only by caste laws but also by cast conventions or associations known as Jati Panchayats.

Caste Functions:

1. It continued the age-old traditional social organisation.

2. It has enabled multiple castes to ensure their livelihood by remaining in their hereditary occupations.

3. Provided social security and social recognition to individuals in their communities.

4. It transmitted knowledge and skills for generations based on hereditary occupations.

5. It has played the role of socialising its community with its culture, beliefs, and values from generation to generation.

6. It provided political stability as it enabled the Kshatriyas to be rulers without being challenged.

7. It maintained racial purity through endogamy.

8. Retained specialisation of skills and led to the production of goods and economic development.

Caste Dysfunctions.

1. It undermined economic and intellectual development and became a stumbling block to social reforms.

2. It has undermined the efficiency of labour and prevents social and economic mobility.

3. It perpetuates the exploitation of weaker classes, especially untouchables.

4. It opposes real democracy by giving monopoly to upper classes to dominate political system at the expense of lower classes.

5. It has stood in the way of developing national, collective consciousness to integrate the country,

6. It has made the oppressed people convert to other religions, such as Islam and Christianity,

7. It has shackled people to abide by their caste norms and beliefs and opposes modern values and change[17].

The caste system has been immeasurably detrimental to India's Integration, societal equality, unity, growth, and development. It has no redeeming value to it other than being a scourge on the Indian society. Mr Rehna notes caste system exists in Islam as *Ashrafs* (Arabs and Persian who settled in India as Muslim rulers and *Ajlafs* (middle classes); in Christianity in Goa, upper cast converts are known as *Chardos,* Vaishya coverts as *Gauddos,* Sudra convert as *Sudirs,* Dalt convert known as *Mahars,* and *Chamars;* in Buddhism, the caste system is practised in countries in countries like Sri Lanka, Japan, and Tibet, and Sikhism too as Zat(Jati) has some features of caste system. But the Caste system is so entranced that even conversions to other religions did not eliminate it. However, As Mr Rehema points out, India's caste system is unique because it has a cultural continuity that no other country has had and has been merged into a modern religion, making it hard to remove. He further notes India lost a lot of time from changing itself.[18] Besides, there has not been a level movement led by credible leaders collectively calling and working for its elimination.

Mr Narendra Modi, a lifelong member of the RSS and its *pracharak,* is a committed Hindu nationalist who became Prime Minister in 1014 and who got reelected as leader of the BJP. As Prime Minister, he seeks to transform India into Hindu Rashtra on the doctrine of *Hindutva* on the idea of pan-Hinduism by marginalising Muslims and other minorities.

---

[17] Rehna, "Caste System in India"
[18] Ibid.,

Conclusion

We have looked at the origins of caste since the time of the Vedic period of ancient India and its rigid classification of four varnas in addition to another class of people as untouchable with respective obligations and duties mandated by the DeVine Manu code on the principle of karma. We have presented a few theories of the caste system and identified its characteristics, its functions, and dysfunctions. We looked briefly at how the Muslim and the British rulers had handled the caste system. We have mentioned that while some Muslim rulers had dismantled Hindu temples and even sought to convert Hindus to Islam, for the most, they left the caste system untouched, although many Dalits embraced Islam primarily to escape discrimination by the upper-caste Hindus. We showed that the British rulers, in fact, had reinforced the caste system by divide and conquer strategy and had further stratified the Indian c society by classifying the untouchables and the tribal people as SCS and STS and had been partial to the upper class. It was only under Independent India that affirmative programmes were introduced and laws passed abolishing caste and prohibiting atrocities of Dalits by the upper cast. Yet, as we have noted, caste stubbornly remains intact and is impervious to laws and reform movements. In the next chapter, we want to discuss the status of Dalits and Adivasis and present briefly an overview of their socio-economic and political conditions in Independent India.

CHAPTER – 2

The Status of Dalits: A Life of Poverty and Assaults

Dalits means, (oppressed or broken) and Adivasis (scheduled tribes) account for 16% and 8% of India's population, respectively; their socio-economic status is worst even in Independent India, as they remain at the bottom of Indian hierarchical society as outcastes as classified by Manu code, considered as the divine text under which they are ostracised and isolated by caste Hindus written more than 2,000 years ago. Dalits have been consigned to polluting, menial jobs such as cremating and handling dead bodies, removal and skinning of dead animals, removal and cleaning of human fluids and excreta (manual scavenging), and basket weaving. Their socio-economic conic and educational conditions more or less remain till today, even though under Articles 341 and 342 of India's Constitution, Dalits and Adivasis have been reserved 15% and 8% in central and state legislatures, in educational institutions and governmental jobs, respectively. The decades of affirmative action programmes have made only a 5% gain for these marginalised groups in the reservation of jobs in salaried and wage employment. Though untouchability was abolished by the Constitution in 1950, the practice remains intact, especially in villages where more than 60% of the population lives. Scavenging is banned yet is in vogue despite the Modi Government's efforts to end it by providing toilets to every household. Dalits live in segregated areas; they are not allowed to enter Hindu temples or draw water wells or taps owned by caste Hindus; marriages between Dalits are taboo, and Dalits can neither touch caste Hindus nor enter their homes. This is the reality of their life in the Independent of India, although these prohibitions against Dalits have loosened to some degree.

The Practice of Untouchability.

In their seminal paper presented at the Population Association in San Diago, CA, in 2015, Dr On the practice of untouchability in India, Drs. Amit Thorat and Omkar Joshi analysed the Indian Human Development data and provided the details on the practice of untouchability in percentages in terms of variables such as households (rural and urban). Caste, religious group, income, and education etc. For instance, the authors showed that 30% of rural practised untouchability while urban 20; in variable caste, Brahmans practised untouchability (52). Forward (24), OBC (34), Sc (15) and ST (22). It is surprising even victims of untouchability SCS and STS practice untouchability. In the case of religious groups, Hindus practised untouchability (30), Muslims (18), and Christians (5). Buddhists (1) and Jains (35); education had a negative effect on education: illiterate practised it (30), 5-9 class (29), 10-11 class (25), degree (24), in terms of income, poorest (33) and richest (23) and in case of region, it is high in Hills (39), northcentral (40), central (49) and low east (16), west (13), and South (17). In summary, Brahmans, rural households, and Hindus, the poorest, northcentral, and central regions, practice untouchability in greater percentages.[19] Urbanisation, higher income, and a fundamental reform of Hinduism that all human beings are equal might help reduce untouchability. In a poll conducted by Pew Research centre in 2021, a substantial share of Brahmans said they would not accept Dalits as their neighbours, and two-thirds of Dalits said there was no widespread caste discrimination against them. However, eight Indians out of ten living in the central region (82%0 and 35% of Indians in the South said inter-caste marriages should be stopped.[20] Little wonder, children of caste Hindus, when they marry Dalits, are either killed, known as "honour killing," or disowned. This heinous practice against fellow Indians who share the same skin colour and culture, eat the same food and dress the same as the caste Hindus do, but ironically, they remain untouchable. This was not practised even during the time of slavery in the US. This is practised only in India, a supposed Vishwa Guru of the world, according to Modi.

---

[19] Ibid.
, pp.8-15.
[20] Pew Research Center, "Attitdues About Caste in India"June 29, 2021 at https://www.pewreseach.org/religion/202106/29/attitudes-about-religion.

A Perpetual Consignment of the Dalits to the Menial Jobs.

As the US CNN network documentary of April 20, 20, shows, Dalits and Adivasis, who account for 25% of India's 1'4 billion population, have been marginalised for centuries and have long endured isolation, and their segregation worsened during Coronavirus of 2020-21. They have been forced for centuries to be cleaners, manual scavengers, and waste pickers-exposing them to a greater risk of catching the virus. These lower-class people lived in crowded slums and were most exposed to the virus and least able to purchase medicine. The documentary quoted the Human Development Programme's report indicating that half of Adivasis were poor compared to 15% of higher castes. India has 6000,000 villages, and almost every village has a small pocket on its outskirts meant for Dalits. Dalits are forced to take up jobs such as cleaning, manual scavenging, working at brick kilns, and leather-crafting- occupations considered filthy or dishonourable for higher caste people. The sanitation and cleaning work formally and informally employs 5 million people, of which 90% belong to the lowest Dalit subcastes, and they are considered essential services by the Government, requiring the lockdown of the COVID-19 pandemic. And the Dalits were required to work at hospitals and elsewhere. This was another risk of discrimination against Dalits. As CNN notes, on March 26, 2020, Finance minister Nirmala Sitharaman announced that all healthcare workers would be covered by health insurance for three months, and sanitation workers would receive special coverage. $66,000 insurance as part of the Government's %22.5 billion stimulus package. However, to claim it, workers needed an employment ID validating their status as sanitation workers. But did not have those cards. And 22% of sanitation, manual scavengers, and waste pickers did not have the 12-digit biometric identification number, and 33% of them did not possess ration cards to get subsidised food through the public distribution centres. As they lacked these cards, Dalits had no access to health care and subsidised food. Sanitation workers would clean hospitals for 7-8 hours a day, but many of them were not given sufficient gear to protect themselves from the virus, and as such, they risk disease. Yes, they were paid 115 a month. The documentary provides many other heart-wrenching conditions Dalits and Adivasis face.[21] Ironically, the Dalits

---

[21.] "Under India's Caste system. Dalita are Considered Untouchables. The Coronavirus is Intensifying that Slur" *CNN*, April 16, 2020, at https://www.cnn.com/2020/04/15/asia/india-cornavirus-lower-castes-hnk-ind/

and Adivasis, by doing "dirty" work, keep the upper-caste people healthy and their environment clean and tidy so that they can enjoy life. One would have them appreciate and admire the sacrificial life of these Dalits instead of despising them. Dalits' socio-economic conditions have been, as we said earlier, remain as they have been for ages, despite the affirmative action programmes introduced since 1950 to improve their socio-economic status.

The Dismal Socio-economic Conditions

We want to describe the socio-economic conditions of Dalits in terms of some facts and figures, for example, regarding education. Dalits are severely disadvantaged the fact that they were opened to educational opportunities primarily since India's independence. Only 10-20 % can read and write, and only 2-3% of Dalit women are literate when the national literacy rate is about 74%. The education disparity between Dalits and higher castes is far and wide as Dalit children struggle with inequality and discrimination as they are often segregated from the rest of the classroom, and other students often face bullying, ridicule, and insults. Female Dalit students are assigned to clean bathrooms. The poverty among Dalits disproportionately affects them in comparison to other castes. About half of Dalits are living in poverty, and 60% of Dalit children are chronically malnourished. Most of the Dalits work in low-paying jobs, which other castes look down upon.[22] Drs. Amit Thorat Subhadra Thorat presents Dalits' high levels of unemployment in a comparative perspective during the Covid-19 pandemic time 2021-22. They point out the Dalits' "economic standing already suffering from high significant levels of unemployment, predominance of informal work, with lower job. Social security support remains at lower levels than the average; therefore, low levels of consumption expenditure combined with low levels of saving back upon the eve of hurriedly declared and unplanned lockdown of the country by the Modi Government, the economy -saw them completely unprepared for the tragedy that was to unfold." Based on the NSS (National Sample Survey) -PLF (Periodic Labour Force) survey of 1918-19, the authors show a higher percentage of SC workers' unemployment (6.4) compared to the national average of (5.8 %), (5.9%) for higher castes, 5.8%

---

index.html

[22] Hannah Drzewiecki, "Dalit Poverty," *The Borgen Project,* December 18, 2020, at https://borgenproject.org/tag/dalit-pverty

for OBCs, and 4.3% for STs. About 84% of informal workers without any job security were SCs, as compared to 70% for OBCs and 54% for higher castes. In the case of salaried workers, SCs were (63%), OBCs were 60%, and higher castes were 50%. They were all affected by the pandemic. In 1918-19, about 65% of workers in total wage workers in the non-farm sector were without contracts or contracts with less than year contract periods. The share of such workers was highest among SCs (89%. OBCs (86%)), STs (87%), and higher castes (76%). The average daily earnings of SC informal workers were RS. 269, for higher castes (357), OBCs (307). Drs. Throats points out the low wage earnings result in lower consumption expenditure on food, health, and other necessities, and based on the 1918-19 survey, the average monthly per-capita consumption for SCS was Rs.1,717, for higher castes 2, 720, for OBCS 1,960, due to preexisting disadvantages. Dalits suffered much more than upper castes and OBCs during the Covid period.[23] Manish Kumar Rao presents an overview of the Dalits' situation and the challenges they face in social, political, and economic areas. We want to cite a few of them.

1. Though SCS and STS (prevention of atrocities prohibiting discrimination against Dalits at the workplace and ensuring equal pay for equal work, the majority of Dalits continue to work in low-paying manual jobs and face discrimination. The poverty rate among Dalits is 31.1% compared to the national average of 21,2% (NSSO 2019). Caste-based discrimination and prejudice in schools and colleges prevent Dalits from pursuing education, affecting their social and economic mobility. In 2019, the unemployment rate among Dalits was 8.3% compared to the national average of 6.7% (NSSO 2019). Dalits are often subject to violence and abuse and often face difficulties accessing education and healthcare.

2. As many Dalits lack educational and skills training, employment opportunities are limited. This keeps them in low-paying manual labour, and they are more likely to work in informal and seasonal jobs, which provide little security and stability. Dalits are heavily unrepresented in the formal sector, accounting for 6.5% of the total

---

[23] Amit Throat and Sukhddeo Thorat, "employment and Dalit Equation," *Outlook India,* February 11, 2022, at https?www.outlookindia./magazine/story//india-news-employment—and-dalit-equation/305416.

formal sector workforce (NSSO 2015). In 2019, only 10.7% of Dalit households had access to bank loans, compared to the national average of 21.6% (NSSO 2019). Land ownership is a critical factor in one's economic empowerment and upliftment in India. However, Dalits have limited access to land, which has been a major factor in persistent poverty among Dalits. Dalits own only 2.2% of land compared to the national average of 47.9%.

3. Despite reservations, Dalits continue to face significant challenges in the political arena. Their representation in elected positions remains limited, and they are often marginalised in political parties. In 2020, only 3.5% of Dalits had political office compared to the national average of 6.3.%. Dalits who hold political office are often subject to violence and intimidation, making it difficult for them to effectively represent their constituents. The majority of Dalits live in segregated communities lacking basic services such as clean water, sanitation, and health care, affecting their health and hygiene and accounting for 56% of disease and illness(national Commission Safari Charam Charis 2020). The author thinks the introduction of the Mahatma Gandhi National Rural Guarantee Act (MBNRGA, and the National Rural Livelihoods Mission (NRLM providing employment and access to credit, respectively, may alleviate the poverty among Dalits.[24] Dalits continue to face assaults and atrocities increasingly from caste Hindus, especially from the members of the RSS/BJP, and they are emboldened to commit these crimes under their man, Mr Modi, as the head of Government.

The Assaults and Atrocities Against Dalits and Adivasis.

Gautam Subramyam writes that violence is perpetrated against Dalits, who are at the bottom of the rigid hierarchy. Hereditary social stratification under the doctrine of purity and pollution has stood yet again centre stage with the BJP under Modi coming to power in 2014. Four varnas classified by Manu Smriti, Subramanyam notes, atrocities against Dalits are committed, even

---

[24] Manish Kumar Rao, "S0cioeconomic Overview of Dalits in Indai" *Round Table India,* February 19, 2023, at https://www.roundtableindia.co.in/socioeconomic-overview-of-dalits-in-india/

though, as noted earlier, in 1989, the parliament had passed SCS and STS (Prevention of Atrocities Act prohibiting them and mandating punishment for those who commit them. The RSS/BJP activists, especially their vigilantes' assault, kill, and lynch Dalits and Muslims for their eating beef and trading cows as Hindus venerate cows as sacred. In fact, the slaughter of cows has been declared in many states as illegal, especially by the BJP-run governments. The upper-caste Hindu activists assault /Dalits for trying to enter temples and falling in love with upper-caste girls. Subramanyam cites the 2018 report of the National Crime Record Bureau (NCCrb), saying that 42,793 cases- on average, one crime every 15 minutes against Dalits, and the number of cases had increased 66% over the last decade. He cites several incidents of assaults:

1. In September 2018, Pranay Kumar, 25, a Dalit, was hacked in broad daylight in the town of Mirvalaguda, Telangana state, allegedly by Maruti Rao because his daughter Amruta had married Kumar.

2. In 2016, in Una, a town in Gujrat state, seven Dalit family members were tied to an automobile publicly flogged. Stripped and marched naked in the town for allegedly slaughtering a cow when they were actually skinning a dead cow.

3. In 2018, in the state of Jharkhand, a BJP minister gave flowers to six men accused of lynching deaths of Dalits to celebrate their release on bail.

4. Subramanyam cites a poll taken in the US in 2020 in which 25% of Dalits had reported facing verbal or physical assault and 60% experiencing caste-based jokes.

Subramanyam points out the following the Supreme Court decision in

In March 2018, diluting some provisions of the Atrocities Act, restricting police powers, and introducing "safeguards" to protect people accused under the law, Dalits protested and took a nationwide strike on April 2 in which 14 -30 people died and several hundred injured due to clashes between the police and strikers. The strike prompted the parliament to amend the act in October 2019, nullifying the court decision as the BJP was seeking a Dalit vote in the May 2019 elections. The court recalled its decision in October 2019.[25]

Abanti Bose makes several observations about how Dalits are illtreated and assaulted by upper-caste Hindus:

1. "Dalits are relegated to the lowest jobs, and they live in constant fear of being humiliated, beaten, or even being raped by the members of upper castes with impunity to keep them in place. Merely walking in an upper-caste neighbourhood is a life-threatening offence for Dalits."

2. Dalit women are often raped or beaten as a reprisal against family members or relatives for their alleged offence committed against members of upper castes.

3. In the 21st century, The Dalit population is not only denied access to education but also, they are oppressed, tortured, and exploited by the upper-caste population.

4. Bose cites the 2001 Amnesty International report, which said only 5% of attacks on Dalits are registered, and police officers often dismiss at least 30% of rape complaints as false, and they frequently ask or demand bribes and beat up husbands of the victims and intimidate witnesses.

5. Dalit girls, even before they reach puberty, are forced into prostitution through a religious practice known as "devadasi." The girls are married to a deity in a temple, and it is their duty to serve God. They are forced to have sex with upper castes. When they get old, they are sold to an urban brothel.[26]

Citizens for Justice and Peace (CJP) cites numerous attacks on Dalits and Adivasis that occurred in 2021 in several states, and we want to mention those incidents in condensed form. It also cites the NCRB report, which said atrocities had increased by 1.2% in 2021 (50,9000) over 2020(50.291).

---

[25] Gautam Subramanyam, "In India Dalits Feel bottom of the Caste Ladder" *NBC news*, September 13, 2022, at https://www.nbcnews.com/world/inindia-dalits-feel-bottom-caste-ladder.

[26] Abanti Bose, "Condition of Dalits in India" *Pleaders*, February 6, 2021, at https://blog.pleaders.in/condition-dalits-india.

1. In Hassan district of Karnataka, a 13-year-old girl was raped by four people, including a minor (Dec 2021)

2. In Ukeri village of Alwar district in Rajasthan, a Dalit family of six, including three women, was attacked, and burnt its cattle fodder for their alleged setting of fire to Gorakhnath temple. Dec)

3. In Wazirgani, Renu, in UP, an 18-year old Dalit youth was allegedly abused and brutally thrashed for touching food during a wedding function (Dec)

4. In Perundurai, near Erode, Tamil Nadu, six fourth-grade Dalit students at a Government elementary school were forced to clean the toilet and the water tank with bleaching powder (Dec)

5. A man named Jagadeesh Gowda, along with his son, was accused of assaulting 16 Dalits and locking them up for several days in his coffee plantation in Karnataka's Chikkamagluru district (Oct)

6. In the Auraaiya district of UP., a social studies teacher, Ashwini Singh, assaulted a Dalit student, Nikhit Dohre, for allegedly spelling a word wrong during the exam, on account of which the boy died in a hospital.

7. In Lakhimpur district of UP, two sisters of the Dali caste were raped and strangled to death before they were hanged in a tree by the accused men (Sept)

1. In Icholli village of Tikaitnagar, UP, the Headmaster of a school threw a hot meal on a Dalit girl, causing burns on her arm. (Sept)

2. An 11-year-old Dalit boy was beaten by his Headmaster for touching his bike at a pre-secondary school in Balia, UP.

3. A 46-year tribal man, Kishanlal Bheel, from BhoomiyajiKi Ghati in Jodhpur of Rajasthan state, was lynched by a group of people over drawing water from a tube well (Nov)

4. Two Adivasi men were accused of slaughtering cows and were allegedly lynched by a mob of 16-20 men in the Seoni district of MP in May.

5. In Alirapur District of MP, two Adivasi women were allegedly sexually assaulted (Mar)[27]

6. In a village in Ahmednagar of Maharashtra state, four Dali men have allegedly hanged upside from a tree and beaten up with sticks by six persons on suspicion of stealing a goat and some pigeons (NDTV, Aug 27, 2023).

These assaults and hate crimes. Against Dalits and Adivasis indicate how violent some of these upper-caste people have become in committing these inhuman and cruel crimes against their fellow citizens because Manu Smriti has said so, not God, blatantly relegating them and them to a subhuman status. The institutional rights of equality before the law and other parliamentary acts prohibiting atrocities against Dalits and Adivasis evidently do not prevent some upper-caste Hindus from committing these crimes because their sense of superiority and purity purportedly endowed by the divine texts have seeped into their mindset. This false sense of superiority is so deeply and indelibly ingrained in their thinking the upper-caste Hindus are willing to ignore the laws of their land. They commit any number of crimes against their fellow citizens and often go scot-free because of their connections with higher-ups in the Government. It is seldom Mr Modi, the Prime Minister of the nation, denounces these crimes being committed mostly by his RSS and BJP members. Lately, Modi has talked about India taking the leadership role in global affairs as "*Vishwa Guru.*" How *can he* make such an audacious claim when so many atrocities are being committed against his fellow citizens on his watch, when his RSS does not believe in India's Constitution and when he deliberately marginalises Muslims and Dalits by acting more as an authoritarian l than as a democratic leader as described by the media, both at home and abroad. It is like an ostrich putting its head in the sand.

On September 2, Udhayanidhi. Son of Chief Minister M.K. Stalin and minister of Sports and Youth Affairs created an uproar among the Modi Government officials and the BJP. Speaking at the conference of the Tamil Nadu Progressive Writers and Artists Association. Udhayanidhi called for

---

[27] CJP, "2022 A Look Back at Hate Crimes Against Dalits and Adivasis" *CJP,* September 7, 2023, at https://cjp.org.in/2022-a-look-back-at-hate-crimes-against-dalits-and-advasis/

the eradication of Santana Dharma by comparing it to "malaria, Dengue and Covid." BJP Spokesperson Shehzad Poonawala said, "This is nothing less than a genocidal call" 80% of the people of Bharat. Home Minister Amit Shah said Udhayanidhi had insulted the country's" culture, history, and Santana Dharma. " A Supreme Court advocate in Delhi filed a complaint with the police commissioner, saying Dayanidhi's comments presented a clear hate speech. Responding to this criticism, Udhayanidhi Stalin posted a note on X saying, "I never called for the genocide of who are following Sanatana Dharma. Sanatana Dharma is a principle that divides people in the name of caste and religion. Uprooting Sanatana Dharma is upholding humanity and human equality"[28]. He doubled down on his previous statement. Sandeep Yadav defines the meaning of the principle- Sanatana Dharma and explains why it is controversial. He says, Sanatana "is an adjective meaning eternal or unchanging often employed by those Hindus who view their faith as timeless, universal, and immutable. To them, it is the essence or core of Hinduism timeless and universal." Udhayanidhi said that he stands by his statement on principle and quoted prominent leaders such as Ramaswami Naicker and Dr Ambedkar, who had said the same about this principle. For instance, Dr Ambedkar, despite his extraordinary credentials, was humiliated because he was classified as untouchable by this Sanatana Dharma, under which the caste system was eternal and unchangeable. In Dr. Ambedkar's view, Hinduism was not based on reason, morality, and equality. Believing that human beings were created equal, Dr Ambedkar produced a Constitution for Indians, granting them fundamental rights, equality, and fraternity under the law. He was disillusioned with Hinduism; Ambedkar renounced it and embraced Hinduism. Ambedkar burnt the Manu Smriti to express his disgust for the document; he launched the Mahad Satyagraha to assert the right of Dalits to access water in public places and the Kalaram temple entry and introduced ed the Hindi Code Bill. Similarly, Nicker had called on his followers in 1922 to renounce the Manu Smriti; he was against idol worship, fought the dominance of Brahmans in Tamil Nadu and became the inspiration for the founding of DMK, a secular party of Shudras. Ambedkar and Periyar had exposed "the oppressive and the discriminatory nature of

---

[28] Nisha Anand, "Udhayanhidi Slammed over Sanatana Dharma Remarks *Hindustan Times,* September 4, 2023, at https://www.hindustantimes.com/india-news/stalins-son-udhayanidhi-slamed-over-sanatana-dharma—remarks- spoiled-brat—who-said-what-10169372.

Hinduism and its caste system and proposed alliterative visions of society based on rationality, humanism, and democracy"[29]. The RSS/BJP is a Hindu nationalist communal party which believes in caste and in the perpetuation of caste hierarchy, arrogating the RSS leadership primarily to Brahmins. The party headed by Modi is well known for its hatred of minorities and their marginalisation, especially Muslims, by treating them as second-class citizens. The Washington, D.C-based *Hindutva Watch's* report released in September 2023, notes an "escalating trend of anti-Muslim since Modi came to power in 2014" It reports that some 80% of 255 documented incidents of hate speech gatherings occurred in BJP-ruled states and union territories during the first of the year 2023.[30] The BJP/RSS claims Dr

[29] Sandeep Yadav, "The Challenge to Santana Dharma from a Radical Politics of Emanipation," *The Wire,* September 5, 2023, at https://thewire.in/politics/the-challenge-to-sanatana-dharma-from-radical-politics-emancipation.t

[30] Hindutva Watch, "Modi's BJP linked to With Hate SpeechinIndia," *Hindutva Watch,* September 25, 2023, at https:// www.deccanchronicle.com/nation/current-affairs/260923/modis-bjp-linked-with—most-hate-sppech-in-india-report-html.

CHAPTER – 3

Major Religions: Beliefs, Practices and Their Impact on India's Caste System.

We want to briefly identify the basic beliefs, practices of major religions such as Christianity, Islam and Buddhism, and their influence or impact on India's Caste system.

Christianity.: Beliefs, Practices, and its Impact on India.

Beliefs:

Christianity began in the first century AD, although it is an extension of

Of Judaism of the Old Testament of about 1,800 BC. It is the largest religion in the world, with 2.6 billion adherents. Christians believe that God (Jehovah) had called out Abraham, the father of Jews from Ur (Iraq), to go to Cannan and establish his family so that He could bless him and his progeny and also others through him (Genesis 12:1-4). Abraham's progenies were finally led out of bondage in Egypt's cruel Kin Pharaoh led by Moses. Jews eventually established their country in Canaan. According to the Bible, Moses gave his people ten commandments dictated by God, and he also wrote five books of the Bible, known as Torah (or Pentateuch by Christians), which are considered holy by both Jews and Christians. The children of Abraham, Jacob and Moses are called Jews, chosen people by God. while non-Jews are called Gentiles. But as Israelites (Jews) had continued to sin against God under different judges and kings, despite God's repeated punishments and forgiveness, the just and forgiving God promised through His prophets to send His begotten son to the earth to save Jews and the rest of the humanity through His begotten son, the saviour of the world. That saviour was Jesus Christ, born of a virgin birth who was crucified for the remission of the sins of men, rose again on the third day, acceded to Heaven, and came back to establish his thousand reign and thereafter judge the world. This is the core belief system of Christianity. It says those who confess their sins and accept Jesus as their personal Saviour and the Lord are called Christians. During His three-year ministry on earth, Jesus spent most of his time in the company of the downtrodden and outcasts, raising the dead, healing the sick, providing eyesight to the blind, and feeding the hungry. Christ articulated the essence of his mission on earth in His sermon on the Mountain, known as beatitudes (Matthew 5-7), preaching forgiveness of enemies, tolerating persecution, and serving the poor. Jesus had problems only with the Pharisees of that day, who sought to place themselves at the top of society and seek power and wealth, whom Jesus denounced (Matt, chap 23). Christianity is fundamentally a pacifist religion, although its followers distorted it and made it be rapacious. This is why the 19th-century German nihilist philosopher Frederick Nietzsche called it a weak and woman's religion. Jesus enjoined his followers to spread His gospel of peace and salvation to every nook and cranny of the world (Matt 28:16-19). One of his disciples, St Thomas, took the gospel to Kerala, where he was reportedly assassinated by an upper-caste person. Accordingly, His disciples, especially Apostle Paul, took the gospel to Asia Minor and other parts of Europe. The disciples preached the doctrine of triune God -God the Father, God the Son, and God the Spirit God in three persons, yet monotheistic. But what did Jesus' disciples say about men, women, and slavery, and how is it practised by Christians? For example, Apostle Paul says, "There is neither jew nor Greek, slave nor free, male nor free, for you are all one in Christ" (Galatians 3:28). But in Ephesians 5: 22- 23, Paul commands "wives, submit to your husbands as to the Lord. For, the husband is the head of the wife as Christ is head of the church." In 1 Corinthians 14:22, Paul says, "women in everything should remain silent in churches. They are not allowed to speak, but in submission as the law says." In Colossians 3:22, Paul asks, "Slaves, obey your earthly masters, in everything and do it but, not only when their eye is on and to win their favour but with sincerity of heart and reverence to the Lord." One can see some contradictions in Paul's statements. Apostle Peter also asks, "Slaves, submit yourselves to your masters with all respect not only to those who are good and considerate but to those who are harsh, for it is commendable if a man bears up the pain of unjust suffering because he is conscious of God" (1 Peter 2:18-19).

Conservative Christians who consider the Bible as infallible and inerrant take the position that women should take a subordinate role to their husbands, bearing children and taking care of the family as husbands are breadwinners and, therefore, they are heads of the family to guide. For a long time, Conservative Christians justified slavery as biblical. However, moderate, and liberal Christians believe that men and women are created by God and, therefore, equal partners with mutual respect for each other and sharing responsibilities. And point out that slavery should be looked at in the context of the times and that it was not ordained by God or advocated by Christ's disciples. Mike Wills, a conservative theologian, defends a subordinate role of wives and women and backs up his position by quoting copiously both from the Bible. Eve's very creation came from Adam's rib, and she ate the forbidden fruit from the Tree of Knowledge, God, and evil, which brought sin into the world. Wills Contends that God intended woman to be dependent on man and the need of her to submit herself to her husband for protection and his leadership.[31] However, George More points out that St. Paul made these statements both as an Israelite with Jewish heritage and training in AW and as a Roman citizen who upheld slavery, not because he supported slavery or the subordination of women to men. He cites the example of Onesimus, who stole money from his master Philemon, a church leader at Colosse and ran away to Rome, where he became a Christian through Paul's ministry. Pail sent Onesimus back to Philemon, asking him to accept Onesimus as his brother, not as a slave. (Philemon 1:8-22). Moore says the ultimate message of the gospel is God, who is making way for men and women to be free from sin and bondage, a complete liberation.[32] Dr Michal Dinkler argues that Apostle Paul had admiration for Phoebe, a deacon and benefactor and Junia, a prominent woman among the apostles. If one sees contradictions in Pail's statements, Dr Drinker argues one should examine the context of interpretations and the times in which they were made as it may result in different conclusions with respect to these passages.[33] Ms Kristi Woods points out, "women have played vital

---

[31] Mike Wills, "The Rule of women as Revealed from the Old Testment, Truth Magazine, at www.truthmagazine.com/archives/volume39GoTO039034

[32] George Moore, "The Biblr and Slavery: Apologetics" at htps: www.namb.net/apolegetics/resurce/the-bible-and-slavery.

[33] Michal Dinkler< "The bible and Woman: We Need to Talk", Reflections,https.relections.yale.edu/article/resistance-and-blessing—women-ministry-and-yds-/bible—and-wome-we-need-to-talk.

roles in the Bible from Eve to Mary, mother of Jesus and many other women; their stories have inspired and challenged us throughout. While men of the Bible are often remembered for their courage and bravery, women are often overlooked. Yet without women, many of the most important stories of the Bible would not exist." She cites several examples from the Bible of women who played prominent roles, contending that women and men are equal, and that is how God intended.[34]

The Practices

Christianity exhibits both negative and positive practices if one looks at it. For example, white colonists from England America initially 13 colonies and occupied the entire content by defeating the American Indians (Christopher Columbus called them Indians, thinking he arrived in India (,1494-96) in a series of wars and finally relegating them to reservations as well as by defeating Mexico in 1846-48 war. Americans justified the expansion on the principle of "manifest destiny "that God chose them to occupy the new land. In the Declaration of Independence issued on July 4, 1776, Thomas Jefferson, the third President, said eloquently that it was "self-evident that all men are created equal by the creator with inalienable rights" those among others being "life, liberty, and pursuit of happiness." But ironically, America's Founding Fathers put in the Constitution of 1787, calling slaves only as 3/5 of persons. Although they stated in the Constitution that the slave trade would end by 1808, it continued into the 1860s. The slave trade was brutal and inhuman as slaves were snatched from west Africa, chained onto the ships, and brought to American shores in deplorable conditions as they resisted and fought their captors and got themselves droned the sea by the thousands. Slaves who had resisted and fought their captors were drowned by the thousands. Wilberforce, a prominent British slave trader who, after he became a Christian, got himself elected to parliament and persuaded the latter to end the slave trade by 1807. Life for slaves was horrendous, with unbearable suffering and pain. Slaves were often beaten by their White masters; they had to work in the plantation fields picking up cotton 16-20 hours a day; Abusing maids and violating their dignity was not uncommon;

---

[34] Kristi Woods, " What Does the Bible say About Women ? The rRoles& Value", Bible Study Tools,April 11. 2023, at https: www.biblestudytools.com/bible-study—topicla—studies//what-does-the-bible-say-about-women-html

it was illegal to read and write; marriages among slaves were illegal, and their children could be sold to other masters. The first 12 Presidents, except for John Adams and his son John Quincy Adams, had owned slaves. Jefferson had more than 35 slaves and fathered children through his slave maid Sally Simmons. The issue of slavery had divided Americans between northerners-abolitionists and Southerners (11 confederate states-) who supported slavery. The division ultimately led to a civil war (1861-65)) under the presidency of Abraham Lincoln in which the southern states were defeated, costing more than 600.000 on both sides combined. Following the end of the Civil War, three constitutional amendments- 13, 14, and 15 abolishing slavery, granting citizenship and the right to vote, and seeking an elective for black men were approved in 1865, 1868, and 1870, respectively. These amendments enabled black men to be elected to Congress. But with the withdrawal of unionist military governments in 1877 under the presidency of Rutherford Hays, segregation laws known as Jim Crow laws were enacted in the South, introducing - separate schools, separate clinics, separate drinking fountains, separate seating on public bussing and railways; right to vote and seek an elective office was restricted and interracial marriages banned. It was only after the passage of the Civil Rights Act of 1964 and the Voting Rights Act of 1965 under the presidency of Lyndon Johnson from the South (Texas) that segregation ended and black men and black women (the 19th amendment of 1920 gave women right to vote) began to vote and get elected to Congress. In 1967, the US Supreme Court declared that banning interracial marriages in 14 states was illegal. South is called the Bible Belt, and it is dominated by the southern Baptist denomination, the largest Protestant denomination with more than 14 million members. They are called conservative Christians who believe in the literal interpretation of the Bible. In the past, they supported slavery, and only in 1994 did their convention pass seeking Christian forgiveness from blacks and reconciliation. They are pro-life and oppose LBBT; they do not allow women to preach from the pulpit, and in 1968, their convention passed a resolution asking women to "graciously submit themselves to their husbands," which turned off many of their women members. The Catholic church, too, does not allow priesthood to women, and celibacy is mandatory both for nuns and priests. Divorce is prohibited. The conservative or fundamentalist Christians overwhelmingly support Trump, though he is an irreligious person, besides being indicted in four criminal cases with 91 charges. Though the Catholic church reveres Mary, Mother of Christ, as holy and thinks she ascended to Heaven without dying, they do not allow priesthood to women on the premise that Christ had no female disciples. Pedi files among priests have become a serious problem at quite a few Devices. Following the enactment of the Civil Rights and Voting Rights Acts, African Americans achieved quite a bit of progress in socio-economic educational areas. Yet 21% of them live below the poverty line due to centuries of slavery and racism, like Dalits in India under the bandage of caste supremacy of upper-caste Hindus. Dr. Corrnel west, a Black Professor of Philosophy at Harvard University, has compared the Dalit situation to slavery in America. There is still de facto segregation in America. The late Dr Billy Graham, a famous evangelist, said that every Sunday at 11 O'clock, America remains the most segregated place because very few blacks attend White churches. And vice versa. Slaveholders had balanced their Christian faith with the cruel facts of slavery based on the Bible. For instance, they used two favourite texts, one from the Old Testament and another from the New Testament. In the Old Testament, in Genesis 9:18-27, because Ham saw his father Noah drunk naked, he became angry and cursed Ham to be a slave of his other sons, Sham and Japeth. Slavery thus becomes the curse of Ham, the father of Canaanites; and in the New Testament, in Ephesians 6:5-7, Paul urges' slaves to obey your earthly masters with respect and fear, and with sincerity and of heart' just as you would obey Christ. Besides, they said slavery was practised among Israelites and that Jesus was silent on slavery. White Christians justified slavery in the US.[35]

The so-called Christian West colonised most parts of Asia, Africa and South America and established its imperialism for hundreds of years, oppressing the colonised people and robbing their natural resources on the false premise of civilising these people. A small trading company, East India Company, had ended up conquering most of India until it came under the control of the British Government in 1858 following the Indian mutiny in 1857. The first two governors- generals Robert Clive and Warren Hastings were quite brutal. Even the British Government had found Hasting's brutal rule unacceptable and impeached him. Initially, the company did not allow William Carey, a British missionary, to start his work in India. Britain, a

______

[35] Noe, Rae, " How Christian Slaveholders used the Bible to Justify Slavery"Time,February,23, 2018, at ttps:time.com/5171819/Christianity-slavery-book-excerpt.

small country of 13 million in the 18th century, ended up colonising 53 countries in Asia, Africa, and the Caribbean Islands. Under King Leopold 11, Belgium=Congo was conquered, reportedly killing 10 million Congolese in the mid-19th century. France had colonised almost one-third of Africa. When Indians had gathered at Jallianwala Bagh protesting the repressive Rowlett Act in April 1919, under the orders of Gen. Reginald Dyer, 700 hundred Innocent Indians were shot and killed, excluding many hundreds wounded in Amritsar. Although some House Lords members had praised the General, he was forced to resign for the massacre. The noted writer Rudyard Kipling justified British imperialism and its continuity, saying that Brown man was the White man's burden opposing India's independence struggle launched by Mahatma Gandhi. During World War 11, Prime Minister Winston Churchill deliberately let nearly 3 million Bengalis die of starvation without releasing the food grain from downs. Churchill, a racist, had utter contempt for Indians and called them "benighted heathens." He called Mahatma Gandhi a "half-naked fakir." Churchill said he was not elected Prime Minister "to preside over the dissolution of the British empire. He was dead against India's independence. It was the Labour Party Prime Minister Clement Atlee who granted independence to India."

The Impact of Christianity on India

Driven by a sense of call, many missionaries, especially from the US, came to India to establish schools, colleges, hospitals, and orphanages to educate Indians, heal the sick and enable them, especially the downtrodden, to find jobs in both the public and private sector. It was the sacrificial nature of their service and the Christian love and compassion they shared with them that some Dalits embraced Christianity to escape oppression from caste Hindus, although the bulk of them remain Hindus despite being relegated to subhuman status by placing them outside the caste hierarchy. The upper-caste Hindus preferred to send their children to Christian schools where the medium of instruction was English. Most Indian elites come from Christian school backgrounds. That is why they tend to be tolerant and appreciative of Christin's service, unlike the RSS/BJP rank and file, which has emerged as a hate-mongering force of Muslims and Christians. India's many Founding Fathers were Western educated and acculturated with the Western democratic values philosophy that had influenced them to fight for India's freedom, gain independence and give Indians the longest Constitution in the world, giving them fundamental rights to all citizens, which the Hindu nationalist Modi Government seeks to deny to minorities. The British rulers, despite being oppressive, built schools, colleges, and railways, gave the British administrative and judicial system, and sought to integrate India in the pursuit of power and economic interests. These are some of the positive aspects of Christianity that we should not be amiss to acknowledge. Christians are a tiny minority, about less than 3% in India.

Islam: Beliefs, Practices, and Its Impact on India.

Islam is the second largest religion in the world after Christianity, numbering about 1.6 billion people. Islam (submission to Allah) was founded by the Prophet Muhammad in the 7th century in Mecca and Medina, Saudi Arabia, who had received revelations of Allah (God) through His archangel Gabriel for nearly 22 years. These revelations constitute the Quran (recitation), the Holy Book of Muslims, and the followers of Islam. It is a simple faith. One becomes a Muslim by declaring one's faith in Allah and that Muhammad is His Prophet (Shahadah) without going through any ritual. The five core principles of Islam are belief in one God and Muhammad is His Prophet, praying five times a day, fasting a month during Ramadan, giving alms (Zakat), and going on pilgrimage (Haj) to Mecca in one's lifetime. Jihad, some consider it as the 6th principle. In one sense, it means a "struggle or strive" against lust, a spiritual struggle, in another sense. It means "strive and fight" in the cause of Allah, a physical (Q 4.95). Islam opposes forceful conversion (Q 2;256), but at the same time, it permits Muslims to "fight and slay the pagans or unbelievers" (Q 9; 29, 73). Islam prohibits killing. It says if sone one kills someone, It is equal to "killing the whole mankind" (Q5: 32). However, if one disputes Islam (Q 3:60-53) or rejects Allah (Q &: 103), one deserves severe punishment(Q 5: 33). Unlike Jesus Christ and Buddha, excluding Jewish kings and Hindu mythological gods and goddesses, Muhammad was a unique person in that he held three roles: a ruler (in Medina), a military leader, he reportedly led 78 military campaigns-mostly defensive, and deputised 59 other) and a Prophet. After his first wife, Khadija, died, Muhammad took another 11-12 wives, including two Jews and one Christian. Islam considers Jews and

Christians as the "people of the book" and permits four wives if they can be treated equally. Islam reveres Mary highly as the Mother of Christ and Christ as the Prophet but does not consider him God. Neither does it believe that He died on the cross. However, it does believe that he has ascended to Heaven, and he is coming back as Mehdi (saviour) to establish peace and justice on earth. It considers a triune God concept a blasphemy. Nearly 200 verses in the Quran talk about "mercy or forgiveness, and only 20 verses talk about judgement or wrath."[36]

Regarding women, Islam grants similar rights as those given to men (Q 2:228) and considers them created equal (Q 4:2). As Manjir Hosain notes, Islam was the first religion to give women a place of dignity and honour' as "there were discriminations towards women' before it was founded. Islam abolished inhumanity, inequality" towards women. However, Hosain writes in many Muslim societies, they are practising contrary to Islamic principles by following their own cultures and customs, and as such, women are being subject to cultural issues, patriarchal features of their own societies and political oppression. Hosain cites several examples to show how Islam treats women on par with men:

1. Inheritance: As mother and wife, she is entitled to 1/3 of the property (Q 4: 11-12). Besides, parents could distribute property equally between sons and daughters.

2. Marriage: Islam gives equal importance to bride and bridegroom to be a valid marriage; each other should acquiesce to marry, and none is superior.it mandates bridegroom of payment of dowry to the wife with no strings attached, it is her money or property.

3. Divorce. a. Although the husband has the primary power to divorce, the wife may also exercise this right to dissolve her marriage if her husband delegates that authority to his wife, b. If they mutually agree to dissolve their marriage, the wife does not have to recompensate her husband. c. If husband and wife feel aversion, they have the liberty to release each other without any claim over the other.

---

[36] For an overview of Islam, see Mir Zohair Husain, Global Islamic Politics, New Yor. : Longman, 2003, pp. 1-37.

4. Maintenance. A Muslim husband is legally bound to provide maintenance to his wife so long she is truthful and observes lawful orders, and whether she is poor or rich, she will not be considered.[37]

Regarding women wearing a veil or Hijab, some argue it is mandatory as the Prophet asked his wives (12-13) and his believing women to wear outer garments when they go out lest they should be harassed (Q 33: 59). But Ms Anna Piela contends, the Hijab in the sense of head covering appears nowhere in Quron, and where it is used. It is a "curtain" or barrier intended to separate the Prophet's wives from visitors. More generally, Hijab is used to describe modest clothing both for men and women. She contends that in the Hijab verses (Q 24: 30-31), the Arabic words " Khimar" and "Jilbab" are translated variously as "covering," "head scarf," and " outer garment or cloak," respectively. Therefore, she says, this range of definitions leads to varied understandings of the need for head covering, and as such, some say it is mandatory, and others deem it optional.[38] However, this issue has become controversial in Europe, even in India, while it is mandatory in many Middle Eastern countries, especially the Gulf states. On the issue of slavery, although slavery was widely prevalent when the Quran was revealed, there is no single Quranic verse that calls for the abolition of slavery. However, chapter 90 implicitly calls for its abolition. It says, "The righteous will travel on a steep path, and the unrighteous will travel on the other."[39] Sau Arabia abolished slavery only in 1962.

The Practices.

Though, as we have noted, Islam is fundamentally a peaceful religion stressing the equality of women and women, its followers have distorted it much more than perhaps other religions and misused its principles. We want to proffer a few examples:

---

[37] Manjir Hosain, "The Rights of women n Islam and some Misperceptions; An Analysis from Bangladesh Perspective" Beijing Law Review, Vol .aspxpaperid=9585010: nNo.5, December 2019, at https: www.scirp.org/journal/paperinforation.aspx?paperid=96850.

[38] Anna Piela, " Muslim Women and the Politics of the Headscarf" Jstar Daily, April 6, 2022, at https:daily.stor.org/muslim-women-and-the-politics-of -the headscarf/

[39] "Islam and the Question of Slavery" at https://islamfyi.princiton.edu/islam-and -the question-0f-slavry/

Saudi Arabia: Wahabism.

The name Wahabism comes from the name of Muhammad bin Abdal Wahab (1703-93), who gave a literal interpretation of the Quran. His followers are called Wahhabis fundamentalists, Islamists, or Salafists (followers and companions of the Prophet). They advocate rigid adherence to the fundamentals of their faith interpreted literally from the Quron and the Sunnah and actively crusade to impose the Sunnah on society and seek to purge those influences they feel detract or demean Islam. They crusade against prostitution, pornography, the sale or use of drugs and alcohol, gambling, Western music, singing and dancing, fortune-telling, fatalism, and superstition.[40] Wahabism was embraced by the original leader (Emir of Dariya, Nejadi), Muhammad bin Saud, in a pact with Wahab in 1774, and henceforth, Wahhabism became the rigid, inflexible Sunni sect of Sad Arabia through its founder Abdulaziz bin Rahman (Ibn Saud, 1902-53) to the present. The only other country where Wahabism is practised besides perhaps Qatar. The king is the absolute leader. Until recently, there was not even an appointed consultancy council. The Quron is the country's Constitution. Women are prohibited from mingling or working with men or by themselves, and they are required to wear veil from face to feet. About more than a year ago, women have been allowed to drive by the young Prince Muhammad bin Salman (MBS), who is trying to introduce reforms in the country, though being equally repressive. But this is not what Islam advocates. The Prophet Muhammad was a businesswoman and an employee of Khadija before she married him. The Prophet, as Government leader in Medina, had a consultative council and gave a Constitution. The Prophet was monogamous until Khadija's death. He married more than 11 women, presumably to take care of them as they had lost their loved ones in the wars the Prophet had had to fight against his enemies. The Prophet allowed four fives if they were treated equally, which is impossible.

Beginning in the late 1960s, the Sudi monarchy used its oil wealth to propagate its brand of rigid Islam in many parts of the world by funding mosques, madrasas (Islamic schools) and Islamist preachers (mullahs). It funded the Mujahideen (Islamic warriors) to fight the Russians in Afghanistan through Pakistan. Subsequently, the Taliban (Islamic students)

---

[40] Mit Zohar Husain, Global New York: Longman, 2003, p.63.Islamic Politic

who were indoctrinated at Saudi-funded Madrasas in Pakistan were able to seize power in Afghanistan first in 1996 and again in 2021. In November 1979, the Wahabi extremists had laid a seizure of the Grand Holy Mosque, demanding the ouster of the Saudi monarchy for its alleged moderation. The Saudi forces have had to engage the extremists in a bloody to clear them off the mosque at a huge loss of life. The monarchy took a series of harsh measures against the ultra-Wahabi clerics, followed by enforcing the Wahabi-based Shariah law to regain its legitimacy. It was the Wahabi brand of Islam which gave birth to the Muslim Brotherhood in Egypt, Saudi Osama bin's Al Qaeda, the Islamic State of Iraq and Syria (ISIS), Boko Haran in Nigeria and many other terrorist groups in the Middle East and west Asia.

Afghanistan: Taliban

The Taliban came out of Afghanistan. Refugee camps in Pakistan from hundreds of Saudi-funded madrasas in Wahabi intolerant and violent brand of Islam. Following their seizure of power in Afghanistan in 1996, the semi-educated Taliban Imposed a rigid, intolerant brand of Islam, denying women the right to education and work, mandating them to wear burqa, and requiring men to grow long beards. They established a primitive, medieval and obscurant system that was contrary to what Islam stands for and what it advocates. Following their removal by an American invasion in 2001, Afghanistan was restored to moderate governments led first by Presidents Hamid Karzai and then by Ashraf Ghani (2002-21), during which time men and women had enjoyed a great degree of freedom and did relatively well with American and international aid, while the Taliban was fighting American presence in Afghanistan funded and supported by Pakistan's army (Interservice Intelligence Agency-ISI). But with the US withdrawal from Afghanistan in August 2021, the Taliban returned to power and imposed its most repressive Islamist Government again at an unprecedented suffering and deprivation for the Afghan people. As a consequence of its brutal policies, no foreign Government has recognised it except for Pakistan, and it is under severe economic sanctions, plunging more than Afghan people on the brink of starvation and malnutrition. Most Afghans are at the mercy of international humanitarian aid. The Islamist ideologues, who are headquartered in Kandahar, do not care for their people. All that they care about is, it appears, sticking to their fanatic Islamist ideology contrary to what Islam stands for. Pakistan, which has funded and supported the Taliban, is now regretting the fact it has proved a haven to Pakistan Taliban (Tehreek-e-Pakistan Taliban-TTP), which is causing so much grief and suffering to Pakistanis through its indiscriminate killings and suicide bombings. Afghanistan, which has been a moderate country under King Mohammad Zahir Shah (1933-73) and his cousin Mohammad Daoud Khan (1973-79) before it came under communists. It is again Afghanistan's salvation if it can return back to a moderate Government with its traditional Loya Jirga institution.

Iraq and Syria: Islamic State of Iraq and Syria ISIS)

The Islamic State of Iraq and Syria (ISIS) was established in 2014 under the self-declared caliphate of Bakr al Baghdadi of Iraq. It is a murderous jihadist outfit Which had occupied parts of Iraq and Syria. While in occupation of these areas, it committed countless heinous atrocities such as torture, rape. Kidnapping, beheading, murder, plunder etc. In Iraq, it forcefully rounded up wives of the ancient Yadis community and raped them mercilessly.[41] The murderous outfit was finally defeated in March 2019 by US special forces in tandem with European and Kurdish troops. Those who had escaped the death or the capture fled to Afghanistan, where they established their base in Khorasan province (Islamic State -K) and are challenging the Taliban for power. Some remnants are still hiding in Syria. This outfit has absolutely abused Islam. These Jihadists falsely believe they will gain 72 virgins in Paradise if they die as martyrs.

Pakistan: A Multiple Terrorist Groups

Pakistan was once a moderate country after Gen. Zia Ul Haq seized power in a military coup in 1977 by ousting a democratically elected Prime Minister, Zulfikar Ali Bhutto, beginning in 1979, Zia began to transform Pakistan into an Islamist state by introducing the Shariah law and by issuing Hudood ordinances (punishments under Islamic law). He supported the Mujahideen through American funding to fight the Soviet invasion of

---

[41] New York Times, October 3. 2021, at https://www.nytimes.com2021/10/0/world/mideast/ydis

Afghanistan in December 1978 and funded anti-militant groups such as Lashkar-e-Taiba (LET) and Jaish-e-Muhammad (JEM) to fight India in Jammu and Kashmir. Subsequently, several jihadist groups surfaced in Pakistan, including Pakistan Taliban-like mushrooms causing so much havoc in the country and making the country ungovernable and unstable. These outfits reportedly might have killed more than 80,000 Pakistanis. They target Shiites (they account for 14% of the population), a tiny percentage of Christians, Ahmadiyya, and Hindus for murderous activities. They burn churches and temples and often engage in suicide bombings. As mentioned earlier, the Quran 5:32 says if one kills someone, it is killing the whole of mankind. But unfortunately, That is not what jihadists believe in.

Iran: An Oppressive Theocratic Regime (1979-Present)

Ayatollah Khomeini, who led the Iranian revolution, ousted from power the 40-year Muhammad Reza Shah Pahlavi in February 1979, and established the Islamic Republic of clerical theocracy by arrogating to himself and his successors absolute power with a façade of representative Government or with President and parliament (Majlis). Following his death in 1989, Ayatollah Ali Khamenei succeeded as the Imam. The regime is much more repressive than what it was under the Shah in that under the latter's regime, Iranians had enjoyed religious, social, and cultural rights, which they were deprived of under this theocratic regime. The Shah modernised the country, established many universities, and sent hundreds and thousands of students abroad for higher education on scholarships. The theocratic regime uses the moral police to enforce Islamic laws, including the wearing of Hija properly. The regime is propped by the Revolutionary Guard corpse, a separate independent force parallel to the country's military. Protests by students, workers, and political activists demanding freedom and their oppression were ruthlessly put down by the police and the Revolutionary Guards. It has become a regular occurrence, for instance, in September 2022. Twenty-two years ago, a Kurdish lady, Mahsa Amini, died in the of moral police in Tehran allegedly for not wearing her Hijab properly. The death gave rise to months of widespread protests defying the regime, woman cutting their hair and removing their hijabs, joined by men by the thousands. However, the regime attempted to clamp down on the protests with an Iron hand, but not successfully so far, as protests are continuing, however, at a low level. Hundreds of protesters, including teenagers, have been killed, and thousands of them detained. The regime has been under international sanctions for its attempts to become a nuclear power and for its egregious human rights violations. On October 7, the Palestinian Hamas from Gaza infiltrated into Southern Israel and savagely killed, beheaded, and raped innocent Israeli women, children, and older people in the number, close to 1,400, including 260 children, young people who were attending a music festival, besides taking more than 220 Israelis and Americans hostage into Gaza. The Israeli response has been equally brutal and ruthless, cutting off food, fuel and water, firebombing Gaza with missiles, artillery, and bombs indiscriminately, and killing innocent wounding the Palestinians by the thousands (7,000 killed by late October) and destroying their houses and infrastructure which has drawn international condemnation except for west, especially the US. Israel has been an occupying power of the west Bank since 1967, and it has blockaded Gaza even after it withdrew from it in 2005. The Gazans are most the brutalised people both by Hamas, which has been ruling the strip since 2007, and by Israel. Most of them are refugees who fled or were expelled by Israel from their homes in Israel, following the 1948 and 1967 Arab-Israeli wars. They live with aid provided by the UN and the international community. It is reported in the news that the Iranian regime was involved in funding, training the terrorists, and guiding them to infiltrate Southern Israel to perpetrate such horrific and despicable atrocities. Iran has become a rogue state. The regime is least popular in Iran. The clerics in Iran have distorted Islam and even abused it to keep themselves in power. Iranians openly call Ali Khamenei a dictator. Iranians are the most educated and cultured people with a great civilisation, and they do not want to be associated with such an infamous regime. The theocratic experiment has failed. Iranians seek a peaceful change of Government and do not favour another bloody revolution.

Most of the Islamic countries are impervious to democracy except for a few countries such as Indonesia, Malaysia, Tunisia and perhaps Bangladesh, though flawed. Dr Pervez Hoodhood, in his opinion column based on his interview with Dr Ahmet Kuru, author of a book titled *Islam, Authoritarianism and Underdevelopment*, writes, "countries where Muslims are majority have significantly higher levels of violence than others," and "on average lower levels of GNP per-capita, smaller literacy rates, fewer years of schooling, fewer examples of functioning democracy, authoritarianism more common, rates of corruption are higher, and the tax -to-GDP is smaller." Dr. Hoodbhoy quotes Dr. Kuru, saying that Islam was not the cause of the negative results, the fact that during the Islamic Golden Age (9th century to 13th century), Muslim civilisation from Baghdad to Spain had sparked with civilisation and learning. However, around the 11th century, rulers and usurpers discovered the usefulness of clerics in endowing legitimacy to their rule. So, Dr Hoodhood concludes by saying that usurpers and rulers using the clerics in politics was the cause of underdevelopment and violence among Muslim countries and cites Pakistan as an example.[42]

The Impact of Islam on India.

The impact of Islam on India has been profound and long-lasting, the fact that Muslim rulers of foreign lineage have ruled India for more than 900 years. Quite a few of them were repressive and mercurial, perhaps except for the emperor Akbar (1556-1605), whose reign was considered a Golden age during which period India had prospered. Akbar was a tolerant leader who even created an eclectic religion, Din Ilahi (divine religion), although it did not get much traction. Even some upper-caste Hindus had not only served in his cabinet but also embraced Islam. A few Muslim rulers had forced conversions to Islam and had dismantled Hindu temples, although a large number who had embraced Islam were Dalits who did it not only because of its monotheistic egalitarianism and simplicity but also to escape the oppression of the upper-caste Hindus. As Dr Ejaz Ali says, an overwhelming 70 per cent of Indian Muslims come from the depressed castes who had converted to Islam because of its emphasis on "equality and self-respect." In 1994, Dr Ali formed the All India Backward Muslim Morcha (ALBMM), an umbrella group of 40 backward class Muslim organisations to promote their interests.[43] It is no wonder the socio-economic conditions of Muslims are as bad as that of Dalits and even worse. In 2006, the Sachar Commission report showed statistically that the socio-economic conditions were even worse than those of the Dalits; it recommended affirmative

---

[42] Hoodbhoy, "Is Pakistan Unusual", Dawn, October 7, 2023, at https:// www.dawn.com/news1779777/is-pakistan-unusual/

[43] "Dalit Muslims" Out look, January 27, 2022, at https://www.outlookindia.cm/website/story/dalit-muslims/2161444/

action programmes for Muslims along the lines provided for the Dalits. The Man Mohan Singh Government pledged to implement the commission recommendation, but the Modi Government ignored it. On the issue of forced conversions, Mr. Maharaj Ratna gives the example of Kashmir. Under Afghan rulers during 1752-1819, Kashmiri people, especially Kashmiri pandits, were persecuted by the Muslim rulers, forcing them to migrate to places outside Kashmir, and those who had stayed back were forcefully converted to Islam ruthlessly killed.[44] Islam prohibits forced conversion. Nonetheless, Muslim rulers greatly contributed to India's art, architecture, music, poetry, literature, cuisine, and other aspects of Indian culture. Today, India's Muslim population accounts for 14% of India's population, the third largest population after Indonesia and Pakistan, respectively. Most Indian Muslims are peace-loving with moderate liberal perspectives. They have a strong democratic orientation and abhor violence.

Buddhism: Beliefs, Practices, and Its Impact on India

If Communist China were included, Buddhism would be the second largest religion in the world after Christianity. Buddhism was founded in the 6th century by the Nepa-India-born prince Gatum Budha primarily as a reaction to the caste system. Lord Buddha was enlightened while he was meditating under a tree. Between the first and third century AD, Buddhism spread to East Asia and Southeast Asia rapidly. It also spread in India rapidly but was demolished by the revival of Hinduism launched by Guru Shankara Charya in the 9th century. India today has about ten million Buddhists.

The basic teaching of Buddhism includes four truths: existence is suffering; craving attachment is the cause of suffering; cessation of suffering is Nirvana (nothingness); and the eightfold truth ends suffering. The path consists of eight views: right resolve, right speech, right action, right livelihood, right effort, right mindfulness, and right concentration. Buddhism, like Hinduism, sees reality in terms of process (Maya), not in substance. It stresses both monastic orders and lay men to desist from things such as refraining from taking life, stealing, acting unchastely, speaking falsely, and drinking intoxicants. Buddhism has two major sects, Mahayana, which considers Lord Buddha as divine and Hinayana, which considers

---

[44] Maharaj Krishen Ratna, "Afghan Rule ib Kashhmir", at https//kashmit.net/mkratna.6.html.

him a teacher and guide. South Korea, Japan, China, and Vietnam adopted Mahayana, while Sree Lanka, Burma, and Thailand adopted Hinayana. It is a pacifist religion.[45]

Ashwani Abode points out that Buddha was credited with five achievements regarding women:

1. He recognised women's right to join the Sangha.

2. He forced the Sangha to recognise the right of women to be leaders.

3. He held the view that women can develop their own personality independent of male support.

4. He broke the myth of family and the importance of producing male children to attain salvation and

5. He Was the first to recognise the need for women's education and political initiative.[46]

The Practices.

As noted, Buddhism is the predominant region in ln East Asia and Southeast Asia. In fact, where Buddhism is practised, those countries are not only democracies such as Japan, South Korea, Taiwan, and Singapore, but they have also prospered immensely. Even authoritarian states such as Thailand, Cambodia, and Laos, with the exception of Myanmar and communist states such as China and Vietnam, have developed, with the exception of North Korea, and have prospered. Perhaps it has a lot to do with Buddhism's emphasis on equality, unity, and strong work ethics. We want to briefly discuss two countries- Sri Lanka and Myanmar (Burma) where Buddhism has been distorted and misused.

---

[45] "What are the Main Beliefs of Buddhism? "mystic River,at https://mysticriver.com.au/blogs//news/what-are-the-main-beliefs-of Buddhism.

[46] Ashwani Labode, " Women's Participation in Buddhism" Feminism in India,April 22, 2021,, at https://feminisminindia.com/2021/04/22/women-participations-in-buddhism/

Sri Lanka and Tamils.

Sri Lanka, a small country of about 22 million people, is predominantly a Buddhist country with a minority of Tamils, who are mostly Hindus who were brought to Sri Lanka (Ceylon) as indentured labourers to work on the tea plantation in the 1870s. Tamils account for 20% of the country's population. Sri Lanka has been a functioning democracy since its independence from Britain in 1948. Tamils who settled in the northeast part of Sri Lanka did fairly well during the British rule and even after the country's independence initially, as they dominated the bureaucracy. But with the introduction of Sinhalese as the official language in 1956 and as the Government and bureaucracy came under the control of the Sri Lankans combined with Singhalese nationalism, Tamil lost their clout and began to face discrimination. So, in 1983, Tamils began the movement seeking autonomy or independence. However, it turned violent after the founding of the Liberation Tigers of Tamil Eelam (LT E) in 1972, especially after it came under the leadership of. Prabhakaran. Perhaps Tamils were pioneers in suicide bombing. The presence of Indian troops following an agreement between Prime Minister Rajiv Gandi and the Sri Lankan Government in 1987 to restore peace in the country did not last long. In fact, its booms ranged against Mr Gandhi both among Tamils and Singhalese, resulting in his tragic assassination in June 1990 by Tamil Tigers in Chennai.

In 2009, a massive military campaign against the Tamil Tigers under the presidency of Mahinda Rajapaksa (2005-2015) and his brother Gotabaya as defence minister, the Tamil militants, including their leader Prabhakaran, were wiped out. In the campaign, the military killed 7,000, including civilians, and destroyed Tamil houses, temples, and houses, forcing nearly 70,000 of them to flee the areas. Subsequently, the UN denounced the Rajapaksa Government for its indiscriminate killing and destruction and for human rights violations and imposed sanctions. However, The Sri Lankans treated him and his brother as great heroes for vanquishing the Tamils. However, it soon became a pyrrhic victory as the country subsequently plunged into an economic crisis, compelling President Gatobaya Raja Paksha (2015-21) to flee the country in July 2021 as protesters stormed his home and his office. ((he returned home in September). Besides, the Tamil issue remains unresolved. Mr Ranil Wickremesinghe, who assumed the presidency in September 2022, appears to genuinely want to address the Tamil issue, perhaps by federalising the country or in some other way. However, Sri Lankans are divided, and Buddhist monks who have representation in the parliament through their party, the National Heritage Party, are quite influential in Sri Lankan politics. They are anti-Tamil; they supported the military campaign against them in 2009 and opposed autonomy for Tamils.[47] This position, as we have noted, is utterly contrary to what Buddhism preaches and stands for.

Myanmar (Burma) and Rohingya.

Myanmar is another Buddhist country in Southeast Asia of more than 53 million people which gained independence from Britain in January 1948. The democratic experiment in Burma ended in 1958, and ever since, it has been under the most repressive military dictatorships from 1962-2011 and again from 2021-present under various military dictators. Ne Win (1962-88, Gen. Saw Muang 1988-92), Gen Than Shwe (1992-2011), and Min Hlaing (2021-Present). The democratic experiment under the San Suu Kyi of the National League of Democracy that worked from 2011 to 2021, however, still under military supervision, collapsed in January 2021, when the military under Gen. Min Haling sieged power in a military coup. It promised to hold elections after 2023. The people who suffered immensely under the military's brutality are the Rohingya Muslims of Bangladesh origin who have been living in Burma since the 13th century in the Rakhine province. In 1982, the military Government declared the Rohingya as non-citizens, denying them access to education, housing, health care and jobs. In 2017, in a ruthless campaign, the military expelled more than 700,000 from their province, besides killing hundreds of them and burning their houses. Most of them fled to Bangladesh, where they were put in refugee camps and were taken care of under the able leadership of Prime Minister Sheikh Hasina. Only the US, UK, and Canada have imposed economic sanctions on the military junta, but there are none in the region, including India. Though the country is endowed with lots of natural resources, it remains the most impoverished country in Southeast Asia. The long history

---

47. For more detainson the Sri Lankan conflict and the role of monks.see Jaysree Bajorie, " The Sri Lankan Conflict, Council of May 18, 2009, Foreign Relations, at https::www.cfr.org/the-sri-lankan-conflict, and Somini Sen Gupta,, " Sri Lankan Government Finds support from Buddhist Monks, New York Times, February, 25. 2007, at https://wwwnytimes.com/2007/02/25//world/asia.html.

of military rule is the cause of its underdevelopment. The military totally has ignored Buddhist teachings of peace, harmony, equality, and respect for human rights. Ironically, Buddhist monks had incited the killings of Rohingya Muslims.[48]

The Impact of Buddhism on India.

Although Buddha and Buddhism are highly revered personalities and religions, respectively, like Christianity, they did not spread at their birthplace, but they spread widely throughout East and Southeast Asia. India has only a tiny population of about 10 million Buddhists. As mentioned earlier, in 1956, a few months before he died, Dr Ambedkar, an outstanding Dalit leader and architect of India's Constitution, renounced Hinduism and embraced Buddhism with his more than 3000,000 followers and urged the Dalits to do the same, although the bulk of them remain within Hindu faith despite being put outside the caste hierarchy and being oppressed by caste Hindus for centuries. Traditions die hard. Even then, Buddhism remains an attractive religion in India, as it preaches equality, oneness of human dignity, community, peace, and nonviolence. For example, in October 2019, 1,500 in a mass conversion Dalits embraced Buddhism in the city of Ahmadabad, in Mr Modi's state, Gujrat, organised by the Buddha's Light International Association (BLIA) funded by Ven Hsing Yun of Taiwan.[49] Hindus claim Buddhism as its own, and some consider Buddha to be one of the incarnate gods. However, as we mentioned earlier, as Buddhism was spreading rapidly in India in the 9th century AD, Shankara Charya launched a campaign and successfully undercut his influence through his famous Advaita school of thought. Dr Daya Hewapathrira points out that in the name of Hindu revival, between 830 and 960, the ancestors of present Hindus destroyed many Buddhist structures and killed thousands of Buddhist monks and their followers. He cites examples of several Buddhist sites in India that

---

[48] For more details on the treatment of Rohingya by the military and Myanmar Buddhists, see Human Rights Watch, " No Justice, and no Freedom for Rohingya five Years on" Aguot 24, 2022, at https·//www.hrw..com/freedoms/2022/09/08/myanmar-no-justice-no-freedoms-for-rohingya-5-years-on/ and Jason, Szep, Special Report" Buddhist Monks Incite Muslims Killing in Myanmar" at https://www, Rreuters.com/article/us-myanmar-violence-special-report-buddhist -monks- -incite-muslim-killing—in-myanamar/idusBRE 9370AP.

[49] Justin Lithatker, " 1,5000 Dalits Convert to Buddhism Seeking Social Equalkiuty" Buddhistdoor, October 1, 2019 at https://.www2.buddhistdoornet/news/15000-dalits-embrace-buddhusn-seeking-social-equality./

were raised to the ground.[50] Today, the RSS and BJP members righteously denounce Muslim rulers and accuse them of having destroyed many Hindu temples, replacing them with mosques, while their ancestors did the same to Buddhism when born on their own soil.

Conclusion

Hinduism is a polytheistic (33-330 million gods and goddesses) religion with divinely sanctioned discrimination and oppression against Sudras, Especially Dalits, and women; Christianity and Islam are nontheistic and are fundamentally equalitarian. As we have noted, conservatives and moderates/liberals express divided positions with respect to the equality of men, women, and slavery. We have noted Buddhism, though agnostic about God, is the most egalitarian religion. We have discussed briefly the beliefs and practices of Christianity, Islam, and Buddhism and how they have been distorted and even abused by their followers. We have cited a numerous example of how Christians, Muslims and Buddhists have distorted and abused the cardinal principles and beliefs of these great religions. Intrinsically, Christianity, Islam, and Buddhism believe in and advocate the equality of men and women, with varying minor differences. We have also briefly discussed the impact of Christianity and Islam on India's caste system and on the Dalits in terms of negative and positive effects. We have noted how some Dalits had embraced Christianity and Islam to escape oppression and discrimination from the upper-caste Hindus. We have noted that the Christian missionary work in India has been historic and unprecedented, improving the conditions of Dalits and Adivasis in the areas of education, health care and employment. In the next chapter, we will briefly discuss some ways how to end Dalit oppression and the caste system in India so that an egalitarian society can be ushered in.

[50.] Daya Hewaaprathirane " Hindu Violence Against Buddhists and Wanton Destruction Buddhist Sites in India"Lankan Web, December 1, 2017, at https:www.laankanweb.com/news/item/2017/12/01/,

CHAPTER – 4

The Imperatives Needed to End the Dalit Oppression and Caste System

The Dalits and Adivasis, who account for 18% and 9% of India's population, have been the perpetual victims of discrimination and oppression for centuries from the upper-caste Hindus. Even after granting them affirmative action programmes, including political representation in state and state legislatures, as we have noted, it has not made a real dent in raising their socio-economic and educational conditions for the bulk of the population. Dalits still suffer segregated lives.; they are discriminated against in education, health care, and employment; most of them are committed to menial jobs and farm labour work. Even highly educated Dalit doctors, IAS officers, and politicians are prohibited from Hindu temples by the semi-literate Brahmin priests and entering the homes of upper-caste Hindus on the notion of their superiority. Even though Dalits and Adivasis are granted equal rights on par with other upper-caste Hindus., and the caste system is abolished by the Constitution, Dalits continue to suffer discrimination, oppression and even untouchability sanctioned by the caste system. The fundamental reason is, as Karl Marx said, those who control the substratum control the superstructure. That is, those e who control social customs, social values, and culture at the societal level (substructure) also control the Government, its institutions, and laws (superstructure). Hence, the societal hierarchy and oppression of Dalits persists despite equal rights granted to them by the Constitution. Most Indian rulers and upper bureaucrats (babus) come from upper-caste backgrounds, and therefore, they control the Government and its institutions and laws. They can choose to ignore the enforcement of constitutional rights guaranteed to Dalits and other minorities with no accountability. Hence, the conditions of the Dalits and Adivasis of discrimination and oppression by the upper strata of society continue unabated.

In 2009, Destitute Children, or Women and Children (NGOs) and the National Institute of Public Cooperation and Child Development(NIIPCCD) published a directory of voluntary No- Governmental Organisations (NGOs) working in different states of union among the Dalits and Adivasis toward improving their social development in the areas of nutrition, child welfare, social welfare, women welfare, destitute children, street children, Child labour, etc.[51] Samar Hafeez identifies five top NGOs fighting for social justice in India. They are as follows:

NGOs and Their Functions

Jan Sahas Social Development Society.

Starting in 2,000, it focused on community empowerment to end manual scavenging, eliminate forced labour, and end gender, caste, and sexual violence. It supports most marginalised groups. It is working in the states of MP, Rajasthan, UP, Maharashtra, and Bihar.

Centre for Social Action.

It works with community-based organisations to develop awareness of the social problems of vulnerable groups of children and women and to respond with various resources to solve them. Some of their initiatives include providing supplementary classes across the districts of Mumbai, Thane, and Raigad with a goal of lowering school dropout rates, enhancing their learning through a plat a method of teaching and improving the functioning of schools by training parents in parent-teacher meetings.

Tilijala Society for Human and Educational Development.

A grass-roots organisation that has been working for the marginal zed and underprivileged people of Kolkata for at least 30 years. It works to empower and transform the lives of rag pickers and their families who have been neglected and socially ostracised, like child labourers and street dwellers. It

---

[51] "Directory of Voluntary Organizations, Scheduled Castes" Documentation Center for Women and Children and National Institute of Public Cooperation and Child Development, 2009, Siri Institutional Area, Delhi10016

also works with vulnerable poorest of the poor, and squatter camps in city who lack even the necessities like drinking water sanitation.

Centre for Youth and Social Development.

The mission of this organisation is to t enable the marginalised to improve their life. It works with tribal communities and rural poor in Odisha to eradicate extreme poverty.

The Humsafar Trust.

The HST is a community-based organisation working on the health and human rights of LGBTQ people since 1994. Through targeted HIV intravenous and they currently reach out to 7,500LGBTQ communities in Mumbai. They also undertake numerous advocacy activities focused on LGBTQ rights. It builds capacities of organisations in 27 states on HIV prevention, treatment, care, and support and advocacy for LGBTQ rights.[52]

There is no denying the fact that the scores of NGOs identified in the directory, and the other five top ones mentioned above, are rendering a yeoman service to improve thousands of marginalised and underprivileged Dalits and the poor as complementary agents of change to governmental welfare programmes. Yet, the NGOs face a humongous problem in India, where 800 million people live in poverty with a lack of health care, education, housing, sanitation, and jobs. There are too many problems for NGOs to be able to address given their limited financial resources, and that is also true at a time when the Modi Government has turned hostile to NGOs by banning foreign funds and even delicensing hundreds of them.[53] In 1949, when China came under Mao Zedong, its GDP was equal to India's GDP. Today. China's GDP of about 17 trillion, six times larger than India's, has become the second largest economy in the world; it has almost eradicated its poverty and has emerged as a superpower challenging the US for influence and power, while India's GDP is just $3.5 trillion having 800 million people living in poverty and depending on Government's doles.

---

[52] Samar Hafeez, "5 Top NGOS Fighting for Social Justice in India'. Give's Blog, February 20, 2021, at https://give.do/blog/5-top-ngos-fighting-for-social-justice-in-india/

[53] Rohini Mohan, "Narendra Modi's Crackdown on CivilSociety in India", New York Times,January 9, 2017, at hrrps:www.nytimes.com/2017/01/09/opinion/Narendra-modi- cracks-down-on-civil-society-in-india.html

India perhaps has the third largest scientific manpower with many natural resources and a much larger cultivable land than China's. It also has a democracy where citizens can be innovative and creative to move on in their individual pursuits freely by unleashing their skills and talents. Yet, India lags far behind China. In a $135 billion trade with China for 2021, India has incurred a deficit of nearly 69 billion. Besides, China has become a threat to India's security land and its territorial integrity, the fact it still occupies parts of East Ladakh and claims the state of Aruna chap Pradesh. It was its unprecedented economic growth that enabled China to build its military power and thus become an aggressive power in Asia. But the question arises: what explains such a huge economic gap between China and India? I would contend that it is the caste system, which is the primary cause, as it has divided people, creating multiple identities and mutual antagonism with no sense of community, unity, and homogeneity. The caste system. It is extremely discriminatory s. It has relegated by Shudras, especially Dalits by relegating them to the lowest rung of society and declared them to fit only for menial jobs by Cleverly using the concept of karma so that they will accept their dehumanised status and never challenge the entrenched powers. Untouchability is the worst of discrimination, which was not even practised by White slave masters in the US. The caste system impedes social mobility and creates a sense of community; it creates the most debilitating feeling of inferiority complex among the Sudras classes, especially among Dalits and tribals, and It divides people inextricably. This is why India still suffers from fissiparous tendencies. As the saying goes, a house divided against itself cannot stand, and India divided cannot develop and become a great nation. The caste system has empowered the upper casts to marginalise Muslims and lynch them and the Dalits in the name of cow protection, accusing these groups of eating beef and trading cows. But ironically, the same people desperately try to send their children to the beef eating west in pursuit of higher education and high-paying jobs. In fact, children of the first and second generations of upper-caste Hindus living in the west have no qualms whatsoever about eating beef. The late Damodaran Sanjeeviah, a prominent Dalit leader, Chief Minister of former Andhra Pradesh state and central minister in the 1960s, would say a cow command more respect than a harijan among the caste Hindus. So, the solution is the caste system, which is a cancer of the Indian society and which metamorphosises in so many ways, should be abolished to end India's fragmentation and divisions and transform the country into a fully integrated, unified, and egalitarian society. The affirmative action programmes put in place temporarily have not cured the problems facing the Dalits and Adivasis. As Amit Thorat and Omkar Joshi point out, reservations have led to only a 5%-point gain in Dalits and Adivasis's salaried and wage employment. The preservations for SCs have become only a band-aid, not a cure. The caste system has given to several caste-based regional political parties, and some of them have evolved into family dynastic rules. The word "Dalit" has become a stigma and liability for the Dalit people. The moment one is identified as Dali, one is looked down upon with disdain and segregated overtly or covertly as if they are alien beings by the upper castes-both educated and uneducated. The permanent cure is the abolition of the caste system. We suggest the following measures or proposals to eradicate it as a belief system and in practice. It is an evil system. However, it does not die immediately. It is a long process which may take decades to disappear. One must adopt long-term and short-term measures to end this dehumanising practice, a scourge on Indian society. Dr Ambedkar emphatically and unequivocally terms called for its eradication in his 1936 book titled Anhelation of Caste (1936) by expressing his righteous anger and disgust over the discrimination and oppression of millions of Dalits and himself as Mahar Dalit by the upper-caste Hindus. They invoked the ancient scriptures to perpetuate discrimination, inequality, and oppression of the Dalits. Ambedkar blames the scriptures for this social hierarchy and for cosigning the Dalits to a state of perpetual degradation as untouchables. In writing this book and publishing it himself, Dr Ambedkar had the moral courage and scholarship to challenge the entrenched social system and was willing to enter the loins den for criticism and rejection by the upper castes. Even Mahatma Gandhi could not call for the elimination of the caste system and criticised Dr Ambedkar for his call for the eradication of the caste system. Although the Christian West, especially the US, had justified t slavery and colonialism in the past. Today no Christian defends them based on the Bible and race except for KKK and some Nazi groups in US and Europe. Perhaps Dr Ambedkar's book should be made accessible to the upholders of this unnatural caste system to shame them and recognise how abhorrent this system is to human dignity and human decency. KBS Sidhu, Special Chief Secretary, Punjab State (2021), identifies and discusses the benefits of abolishing the caste system, stating that it promotes social cohesion, creates a merit-based society, ensures equal access to opportunities, eliminates caste-based discrimination, and promotes human rights and dignity. He also discusses points against abolishing laws based on caste, including reservations.[54] Darpan Singh noted the Supreme Court in 2018. asked states and the centre not to use the word "Dalit" as it has become abusive and offensive. Singh writes, "Many of the politicians who rose to power claiming to champaign the cause of scheduled castes, scheduled tribes or Other Backward Classes have focused on accumulating wealth and promoting their own, instead for the masses and changing the situation on the ground" for the Dalits who are in the awful condition of life. Mr. Singh quotes the former late President Abdul Kalam, who advocated that the Government must provide urban amenities in rural areas to end social inequalities, increase college seats substantially and job opportunities, and address social tensions. The author concludes his article by saying, "Authorities must do their job to prevent discrimination, oppression, violence, and act against offenders"[55] The urbanisation of rural areas, increased college seats and job opportunities may be a partial solution, but the primary cause of India's sectorial economic iniquities is the entrenched and perpetual caste system which has to end for India to become an egalitarian and globally respected country. There is an urgent need for a grass-level-based national movement calling for the eradication of the caste system in India. Occasionally, some politicians or groups may call for its education, but it seldom gets traction among Indians, and the call dissipates quickly. For example, Rajendra Pal Gautam, minister of Social Welfare in the Aam Admi Party (AAP) Government, resigned over a conversion tussle between the AAP and BJP and took out a march in New Delhi joined by a thousand people on October 5, 2022, commemorating the day of October 5, 1956, when Dr Ambedkar and his followers had embraced Buddhism and called for eliminating caste system and unity within the community. He called his march "caste Elimination Sankalp Yatra."[56] The following are

---

[54] RBS Sidhu, "Abolishing Caste System in India: Propositios and Perspectives", Medium, March 18, 2021, at https://kbssidhu1961.medium.com/abolising-caste-system-in-india-prpositions perspectivesfb1fb5bae8b8.

[55] Darpan Singh, "Whis Dalit Savama? Why Caste System must go in Totally "India Today, August 8, 2022,, at https://www.indiatoday.in.newa-analysis/story.dalit-savama-caste-system--must-go-1989509-2022-08-18.

[56] Mayank Paracha, " Converting Dalits to Buddhism is not a new Phenomenon But Continues to Agitate BJP" Outlook India,October 8,2022, at https:www.outlookindia.com/national/converting-dalits-to Buddhism-not-a-new-phenomenon—but continues-to-agitate-bjp.

some proposals for consideration by leaders and groups who seek to end the caste system.

Starting a National Caste Eradication Movement.

There is a need for a national caste eradication movement headed by a credible, charismatic, and well-educated person with knowledge of the Hindu scriptures dedicated to the elimination of the caste system. Knowledge of the Hindu scriptures will enable him or her to effectively debate those who defend the status quo caste system. He/she could come from any caste so long that person is dedicated to the annihilation of the caste system. In addition, there should be state, district, mandal and village-level branches to work in tandem with the national movement. The movement should persuade the centre and state governments to make laws there was no discrimination and oppression of the Dalits and Adivasis and to make sure those who commit such crimes are punished severely regardless of that person's status in society. The movement should assume the watchdog functions to make sure Dalits and Adivasis are integrated fully into every area of society.

Although forward classes and other word classes, along with SCs, STs enjoy reservations at 10%, 27%, 15% and 8%, respectively, it is always Dalits who are singled out and stigmatised as people underserved, enjoying these advantages, especially in professional schools admissions. Even at the state level and central ministries, Dalits and Adivasis are given a token of 1-2 peripheral ministries representing their communities. As such, the issue of caste-based reservation has become a liability, not an asset, when they make only a 5% per cent [point gain in salaried and wage employment. Therefore, so long the affirmative action programmes are in force, they should be based on socio-economic and historical factors, not on caste. One's caste should not be mentioned on job or admission applications. Given very low-level socio-economic factors, Dalits and Adivasis are likely to be eligible for these programmes without mentioning their caste.

Dalits and Adivasis will consider voting only for Secular Parties to protect their rights.

The Founding Fathers of India, with a broad vision, gave a secular Constitution granting fundamental rights to all citizens to meet the imperatives of a mullet ethnic and multi-religious India. The Congress Party, which had dominated India as the ruling party for more than 30 years, sustained India's secular principles while protecting the rights and interests of minorities which the BJP considers Congress's commitment as appeasement and to protect its vote banks and called its espousal of secularism contemptuously as pseudo-secularism. Although Brahmans are blamed for the persistence of the caste system and for the caste-based discrimination against Dalits, if one looks at the treatment of Dalits objectively, they did much better under governments headed by Brahman Prime Ministers., Their rights and interests were protected under Brahman Prime Ministers: Nehru, Lal Bahadur Shastri, Indira Gandhi, Rajiv,\Gandhi, Morarji Desai, P..V, Narasimha Rao. Even Atul Behari Vajpayee, though an RSS member, had abandoned Hindutva and had worked for the common weal of all Indians, including Muslims and Dalits. As a statesman scholar with a broad vision, Vajpayee sought to build better relations with Pakistan, even visiting the latter twice as Prime Minister. We seldom heard of Muslims and Dalits being lynched for alleged beef eating and cattle trading under the previous prime ministers except under the Modi regime, dominated by Hindu nationalism, though he comes from humble beginnings of another backward class background.

Mr. Modi has been an RSS Pracha Rak (promoter) throughout his adult life. In 2001, Modi was appointed Chief Minister of Gujrat by Prime Minister Vajpayee; four months later, following Hindu riots against Muslims in which he was implicated, Modi used the mayhem against Muslims as an asset to win a landslide victory though banned from visiting the west until 2014 when he became Prime Minister. By promising better and cleaner governance economic development, Modi won a landslide victory for his BJP in 2014, and when his policies like demonetisation and GST (Goods and Services Tax), among others, became unpopular, Modi used the Pakistan-sponsored terrorist attack on a military convoy in Kashmir to zin up national outrage and won again a landslide victory to remain in power. As the BJP has appropriated Dr Ambedkar as its own (though it hardly believes in a scintilla of what he stood for) and lured by respectively his promises of jobs, Dalits voted for his party by 27% and 30% in 2014 and 2019 by abandoning their favourite Congress Party not realising the devastating consequences for them and Muslims. Aa RSS and BJP believe in caste-based social hierarchy and the establishment of the Hindu Rashtra based on the Hindutva ideology of Hindu supremacy and the Manu code; Modi deliberately began to marginalise Muslims. It passed the Citizenship Amendment Act (CAA) in 2019 and promised in 2021 to enforce the National Register of Citizens for the whole country besides the state of Assam; it abrogated Article 370. 35 A, under which   J&K had enjoyed Special status arbitrarily in 2019, and its RSS vigilantes, such as Bajrang Dal and others, began to lynch Muslims and Dalits for eating beef and for alleged trading of cattle. Some of the Hindu Priests at t their gatherings openly called for Muslim genocide and raping of Muslim women. But Modi never denounced such people by giving them the perception that he was the Prime Minister only for Hindus. Not even one Muslim is in Modi's cabinet or an MP belonging to his party. He has muzzled the media; he does not countenance any criticism of the regime, and one finds himself or herself in jail and uses governmental investigatory agencies to punish opposition politicians or to intimidate them into defecting to his party. The BJP is a communal and sectarian party, and if Dalits or Adivasis continue to note such hate-spewing parties, they are doing it at their own peril for them and Muslims. They ought to consider voting for men and women with impeccable character and commitment to secularism. They could use social media and the internet to figure out if the candidate was a person of integrity and character before they vote. Mr Modi never misses a day criticising the Congress Party as corrupt and Rhul Gandh's leadership as part of a family dynasty, although Mr Gandhi is a highly educated person from Cambridge with superb credentials. Modi promised a clean Government and his party MPs would be persons of character and integrity. However, according to the Association of Democratic Reforms (ADR), 116 (39%) BJP MPS elected to Lok Sabha in 2019 have criminal record cases against them.[57] According to Transparency International, India ranks 85 on the

---

[57] "43% newl Elected Lok Sabha MPS have Criminal Record: ADR" The HinduMay26, 2019, at https://www.thehindu.com/elections/lok-sabha-2019/43-newly-elected-lok-sabha-mps--have-criminal-record-adr/artcle27253649.ece#-rext=havecrim.

Corruption Perception Index out of 180 countries (0 being very corrupt and 100 being clean).

If the STS and Muslims, who account for 18%, 9% and 15%, respectively, vote for any credible secular and mass-based political party, it is unlikely they will be allowed to l suffer this humiliation, discrimination and lynching under such parties, and they are likely to be treated with dignity and respect enjoying fundamental rights as full citizens, and there will be no "love Jihad" laws outlawing inter-faith marriages., and India will be restored to its secular status as envisaged by the India's framers of the Constitution. The destiny of minorities is with secular parties, not with divisive communal parties.

Promote Inter-caste Marriages.

One speedy way of eradicating the caste system is by prompting inter-caste marriages on a massive scale. This is what Dr Ambedkar has advocated as a way to eradicate caste hierarchy. As of today, only 10% of marriages are inter-caste. Most of the marriages in India are arranged by parents or close relatives. One reads about ostracism, harassment and even "honour killing" if one's daughter or son enters an inter-caste marriage alliance, especially with Dalits. NGOs and Dalit leadership ought to promote inter-caste marriages and persuade both central and state governments to provide incentives such as jobs, housing, and educational opportunities for such couples. Special courts should be empowered to give swift and proportionate punishment for those who harass, ostracise, or hurt for entering inter-caste marriages. State governments and even the central Government should be persuaded to create a cabinet rank to promote these marriages. Even though the dowry system has been abolished, it is still practised. Parents and their daughters should be persuaded not to marry anyone who demands a dowry. It is a bad and costly practice for parents, and there are mysterious dowdy-related deaths. As the famous civil rights leader in the US, Dr Martin Luther King, had said, one should be judged based on the content of character, not on the colour of the skin. It is not the man-made caste, but it is the character and integrity of a person which should be the basis for entering into marriage. Such marriages will be fulfilling, enriching, harmonious, dignified, and self-respecting.

Promote an Integrated Housing

When the state and central governments embark on building housing complexes for underprivileged classes, Dalits and Adivasis, NGOs and the Dalit leadership should insist on integrated housing encompassing all castes as one way of making them live together and help them cultivate a sense of community transcending caste barriers. Only people who accept such a requirement should be allocated housing. This will be another effective method of ending the segregation of Dalits from other caste communities. It is not only Dalits and Adivasis who live in huts, mud, and thatched houses; so do many backward classes who badly need better housing who should be willing to join integrated housing.

Generate Alternative means of livelihood for Dalits and Adivasis.

It is an indictment of the Indian democracy that even after its 76 years of independence, the bulk of Dalits and Adivasis are forced to do menial jobs, including the most dehumanising job of scavenging in many parts of India. One good, noteworthy thing the Modi Government has done is on the issue of sanitation. It seeks to provide toilets for all families. This policy cannot succeed unless all poor Indians have proper housing and access to water, electricity, and employment to pay for the utilities. Besides, many Indians defecate outside their homes, and using toilets (It is said that 60% of them defecate outside their homes) is a new experience for some of them. Old habits die hard. The Dalit leadership, NGOs, and governments should work together to open up other alternative avenues of livelihood for Dalits. Dalit Adivasis have suffered for ages doing these menial jobs, exposing them to all kinds of ailments; The centre and state governments have an obligation to help Dalits and Adivasis find alternative jobs, including granting some of them ownership 1-2 acres of Government land to enable them to cultivate and earn their livelihood. They should be provided with small loans from Grameen and state banks to enable them to explore new job opportunities themselves. Even the World Bank could play a role in this endeavour. The Modi Government has spent/spending close to $ 2 billion on the central Vista Development project, including a palatial Prime Minister's house. This amount could have been used to help Dalits and Adivasis find alternative jobs to gain a dignified life. This is an example of misplaced priorities for the

Modi Government. Dalits and Adivasis should vote only for those parties and politicians who are genuinely willing to ameliorate their depressing conditions, not for those who engage in election gimmicks to win power.

Encourage the Dalit Youth to Join the Police Force and Become Lawyers.

The Indian population is corrupt to the core, dominated by caste Hindus. Consequently, when Dalits are discriminated against, harassed, lynched, and their women's dignity is violated by caste Hindus, oftentimes, the culprits go scot-free because Dalits are afraid to report to the police, fearing reprisal and also they fear t that the police may not take up their complaints perhaps for reasons of acceptance of bribes or political pressure from the higher-ups. Therefore, there is a dire need for Dalits to join the police and for Dalit lawyers to fight for equal justice under the law. Their presence in police and lawyers to fight their cases even on a free bona basis may embolden the afflicted Dalits and Adivasis to confront the oppressors. Dalits should be encouraged to take and pass necessary exams to join special courts to help render equal justice regardless of one's caste and creed.

Encourage the Dalit Youth to Join the Priesthood.

Until today, the Hindu priesthood has become the prerogative of Brahmans. It need not be. Anyone who has the desire and a calling to be a priest ought to be given the opportunity to train himself and become a priest, as is the case in Christianity, Islam, and Buddhism. In fact, the DMK Government in Tamil Nadu recruits young people from backward classes and Dalits and trains them to become priests. This practice could be emulated by every state to train the youth from backward classes and Dalits to become priests. This is another way of bringing equality among all castes- no one is superior or inferior or inferior- all are equal.

Promote the Spread of Buddhism.

As we have noted, among all religions, Buddhism is the most egalitarian religion, emphasising equality among all men and women, nonviolence, tolerance, and brotherhood of humanity. This is Why Dr Ambedkar and men of his stature have embraced Buddhism and asked others to follow suit. Of course, faith is based on one's belief and conviction and no one should compel or force anyone to embrace a particular religion. However, one should not hesitate to propagate one's religion's principles and beliefs, which are the rights granted by the Constitution. The famous German nihilist philosopher Frederick Nietzsche admired Buddhism among all religions.

Promote Hindi as a national Language to Integrate Indians.

A national language is a powerful unifying and integrating vehicle for any nation. It creates an emotional attachment to a nation. For example, America is a multiethnic nation consisting of nearly 180 ethnicities and is multi-religious. Yet, there is a strong sense of Americanness among all these groups because of the language- English has been used as a unifying instrument. These groups consider themselves as Americans first and last because of one language, both as a language of communication and as an official language, although English is not mentioned in the US Constitution to be a national language. Hispanics account for 14% of the population, and once they are here, they learn English and make their children proficient enough to be able to make it in the US. Indians often define themselves in linguistic and state terms as Tamils, Malayalam, Maharashtrians, Gujaratis, etc., but not as Indians. These days, the Modi Government want to replace the name India with Bharat. The framers of the Indian Constitution wanted Hindi as a national language. As it is, nearly 60% of Indians know Hindi in varying degrees of proficiency. Even the Dravidian languages of the South have more than 70% Sanskrit-based words. Except for Tamil Nadu, there is no opposition in the South for learning Hindi. Of course, regional languages have their rich poetry and literature. Nonetheless, in the interests of creating emotional integrity, all Indians should be persuaded to learn Hindi as a language of communication, but not forced by providing incentives to learn Hindi. Dalit leadership could play a positive role in this regard. States created based on language have engendered sub-nationalism and even irredentism, ultimately leading to fissiparous tendencies as we have witnessed in Punjab, Assam, and Nagaland. India has suffered from hundreds of foreign rule and colonialism, and we cannot afford to be divided due to the lack of one national language.

The Need for a National Organisation to Deal with the Threat of the RSS

Once treated as a pariah and implicated in the assassination of the Father of the nation, Mahatma Gandhi, the RSS today has emerged as the most powerful organisation in India, as Sangh Parivar with more than 30 ancillary units. It has fathered the BJP, which has become the dominant ruling party both at the centre and among many states of the union since 2014. As the former RSS chief and idealogue, MS Golwalkar (1940-73) advocated, it believes in the social hierarchy and in the Manu code, with Brahmans as spiritual advisers and guides at the top of the caste hierarchy. It believes in relegating Dalits and women to a degrading status as stipulated by Manu Smriti. It treats Muslims disparagingly and seeks to marginalise them as if they are not full citizens and as foreigners unless they reconvert themselves to Hinduism. Its adherents openly call for their genocide and engage in lynching them and Dalits for beef eating with no accountability. It is a most divisive, polarising entity and poses a threat to India's unity and integrity, a multi-religious country. Unless there is a countervailing organisation at the grass-roots level undergirded by Dalits, Adivasis, and secular Hindu Groups and is willing to deal with this menace, the RSS and its branches may cause India to fragment based on religion and caste. The RSS wanted to establish a Hindu Rashtra to the exclusion of minorities as Adolf Hitler had sought to establish a thousand-year Reich and had started the Second World War in search of lebensraum for Germans. In fact, the RSS founders had admired the Nazis and the Italian fascists. The RSS believes in the racial supremacy of upper castes as Aryans. It stresses the prerogative of a Brahman to be the RSS Chief. At close on the eve of elections in UP in August 2016, the then BJP President Amit Shah, now Home Minister, had dined with a Dalit MP, Kaushal Kishore house in Lucknow, and the RSS Chief Mohan Bhagat had visited Dalit house activist Rajendra Singh's house in Agra and had lunch with him. The opposition parties termed their dining with Dalits as a public stunt, not out of the sincerity of their heart believing in social equality.[58] One wonders if Mr Bhagat had ever invited a Dalit person to his house to dine with him and his family to demonstrate that he believes in social equality of all human beings and a caste-less Indian society. The national

---

58. "RSS Chief Mohan Bhagat Dines with Dalit Activist in Agra", India Today, August 24, 2016, at https://www. inditoday.in/mail-today/story/mohan-bhagat--rss-dines-dines-with-dalit-in-agra337038-2016--08-24.

organisation should consist of scholars, points, journalists, politicians and activists who should be able to confront and debate the destructive and divisive ideology of the RSS/BJP and, at the same educate Indians about the danger posed by the RSS through their lectures, debates, articles and through the social media to wean Indians from such a dangerous outfit most Hindus even those who believe in tradition of caste system, are tolerant people; they do not hate Muslims and Christians, because they belong to other religions. The RSS should remember that it was the oppressive treatment of Dalits which had compelled some Dalits to embrace Islam or Christianity out of their own personal convictions. Americans who are predominantly Christian do not hate or discriminate against other religious groups because they are Hindus, Muslims, Buddhists, and Jews, although a few fringe elements do that. Though BJP won a landslide victory, it only won 30% and 35% of the popular vote. It won such a victory because of the principle first past the post. If the RSS/ BJP does not treat Muslims and Dalits with respect and dignity, entitling them to enjoy the same rights as other Indians and stop lynching them, it may compel Muslims, Christians, and Buddhists who are mostly from Dalit backgrounds to join together to make the country ungovernable. Look at what Naxals, who are mostly from Dalit and Adivasi backgrounds, are doing. Indians of all religions, beliefs, and castes should work together to make India an egalitarian, harmonious, prosperous country, and an exemplary democracy. The RSS is taking its divisive doctrine even to the west, maligning the good name of Indian immigrants who are respected for their tolerance, amiability, and for their significant contributions in the fields of science, medicine, technology, and teaching.

Introduce a Mandatory Civics course at the college level to Enlighten Students.

Philosopher George Santayana said those who forget history are cursed to repeat it. Many Indian students hate learning history, and many of them are not familiar with tolerant history and the eclectic nature of Indian religions. Indians had lived under local feudal rulers, foreign Muslim rulers and the British Raj for hundreds of years, facing oppression, humiliation, and degradation. Hindus, Muslims, Parsees, and Christians had joined Mahatma Gandhi to gain independence and establish India as a Republic under an exceptional Indian Constitution granting all Indians equal rights regardless of their caste. The knowledge of India's struggle and the exceptional nature of the Constitution may make the Indian youth appreciate and admire the Founding Fathers and learn to sustain the institutions they have created so that all Indians can enjoy the blessings of democracy. The youth must learn that Indians do not hate people because some people belong to other religions. They are not hate-spewing discriminatory RSSBJP. The course on civics should be made mandatory for all college students to become enlightened citizens lest they should become prey to the destructive and bigoted philosophy of Hindutva espoused by the RSS/BJP.

India ranks number one in the world with respect to superstitious beliefs. Late Nobel laureate V.S. Naipaul once wrote that Indian nuclear scientists seek astrology and horoscope, And humanist Babu Gogineni reportedly said that Indian scientists are rational so long they are in the labs, but once they out of them and take off their white coats, they return back to their old beliefs and caste practices. This is perhaps due to long-lasting superstitious beliefs implanted in the Indian mind. One wonders if the course on Logic at college will help Indian students   deal with these beliefs

Conclusion

In this chapter, we have suggested some proposals to eradicate the age-old, entrenched caste system and the Dalit oppression and discrimination. We have suggested ways such as the establishment of a national movement calling for the elimination of the caste system, Dalits and minorities considering voting only for secular parties, promoting inter-caste-marriages, opening alternative jobs for Dalits and Adivasis, promoting integrated housing, encouraging the Dalit to join police force and judiciary to assure the underprivileged to obtain fair justice when oppressed by the upper-caste Hindus under the rule of law, promoting Buddhism as way to introduce equality among men and women and finally introducing a civics course at college level help produce enlightened Indian citizenry. Of course, caste will not end suddenly. It is a long process involving decades to get rid of it, But it is worth the effort to redeem Dalits and Adivasi of centuries of discrimination and oppression for the good of India.

CHAPTER – 5

Conclusion: Equality of all men and women.

The 18th century French philosophy [her Jacques Rousseau said, "Man is created free but finds himself in chains everywhere," and as noted elsewhere, the US third President Thomas Jefferson, in the June 1776 Declaration of Independence, said eloquently that all men are created equal by the e creator endowed with certain inalienable rights and those rights among others being "life, liberty and pursuit of happiness." Yet, the US had practised slavery for more than 200 years, and the first ten Presidents had owned hundreds of slaves.

India has been practising the caste system for more than 2,000 years; Indians defend it through an unnatural and irrational practice, stating that it was divinely sanctioned. The 17th-century English philosopher John Locke said when a child id is born, his/her brain is Tabula Rasa, a clean slate. However, as the child grows, he/she is imprinted with ideas of good, bad, and ugly through socialisation agents such as at home, in school, in peer groups, in the church/temple, and on social media. So, if Indians believe and practice for centuries the caste system, it is the work of these agents. Indians have to be disabused to learn that we are created equal by the creator, and therefore, it is incumbent on us to learn to treat each other as equals and brothers and sisters. But it will take decades to unlearn these unequal and degrading practices and transform oneself into a new man and woman.

In the first chapter, we have looked d at the origins of the caste system in ancient India and that Mau Smriti has rigidified the varna system, prescribing their respective duties for different varnas while relating Dalits (Chandolas) to subhuman status fit to do only menial jobs outside the caste hierarchy which become the Bible for the RSS and its political wing -the BJP. We have identified some theories of the caste system and its main elements, as well as the caste system's main features and functions. We have also briefly discussed the foreign rulers- both Muslim and British and how they handled India's caste system. We have pointed out that while Muslim rulers had maintained the status quo of the caste system, other than occasional attempts to convert Hindus to Islam, the British rulers have exacerbated it by choosing winners and losers in support of their colonial rule. It was the British Government which created separate, distinct scheduled castes and scheduled tribes' classes, presumably to provide them with some economic benefits. The British played divide and rule to maintain their grip over the country. We have identified a few reform Hindu reform movements founded as a reaction to a foreign rule to end evil practices such as Sati, child, and untouchability, but their impact on reforming Hindu practices has been minimal. In Chapter 2, we have discussed briefly the persistent pitiful socio-economic and educational conditions of Dalits and Adivasis, their object poverty levels, their dehumanising experience of untouchability even in the 21st century, and perpetually consigning them to do menial jobs. We have also cited several examples of how atrocities, including beef-related lynchings, are being committed by the upper-caste Hindus, often paying no price for those crimes. We have indicated that discrimination and atrocities against Dalits have increased under the Modi regime. In the third chapter, we have identified the main beliefs of major religions such as Christianity, Islam, and Buddhism to provide a comparative perspective with the Hindu caste system with respect to the rights of men and women and slavery and presented a few examples of how these religions have been distorted and even abused. We have also briefly discussed the impact of these religions in India- both positive and negative, and how Dalits have been attracted to these religions to escape upper-caste oppression. In the fourth chapter, we have offered several measures and proposals for consideration to end both the caste system and oppression of Dalits and Adivasis to build India into an egalitarian society where all men and women are treated equally. We have suggested the establishment of a national movement calling for the eradication of the caste system, encouraging the Dalits and Adivasis to vote only for the secular parties to protect their rights and interests, not for BJP, a communal party under which discrimination and atrocities again have been increased; promoting inter-caste marriages and integrated housing as a way to end cast system; encouraging Dalit youth to join the police force and the judiciary as a way to eliminate discrimination by the upper-caste and establish the rule of law and fair justice; promote Buddhism as it is the most egalitarian religion, and establish a national secular organisation to educate Indians about the danger posed by the RSS. The discrimination and oppression of Dalits and Adivasis will not end unless the abhorrent caste system is eradicated for good. Then, equality among all men and women will be established alone.

Mr Modi is radically different from the previous 13 Prime Ministers in that he has been an RSS preshrank throughout his adult life propagating RSS Hindutva philosophy. If Muslims are being marginalised and the number of atrocities against Dalits has increased, perhaps he is incapable of coming out of his cocoon, a narrow mindset of Hindutva and Hindu nationalism. Apparently, Modi does not consider himself the Prime Minister of all Indians regardless of their caste, creed, and religion... He seldom calls himself an Indian nationalist encompassing all Indians-Hindus, Muslims, Sikhs, and Buddhists. Nation-building requires the leader's unqualified dedication and commitment to the common well-being of people regardless of their caste and religion. Mr. Modi wears religion on his sleeves to show his religiosity by dipping himself in the Ganges and by worshipping often at temples or inaugurate temples to appeal to Hindus who are religious. Maybe he is genuinely very religious. Having come from a humble beginning with a backward class background, one would have expected him to transcend religious prejudice and strive for the d good of all Indians. He is known for his prejudicial attitude and disdain for Muslims, who are mostly from Dalit backgrounds, the sons of the soil, not of foreign origin, and living in abject poverty, as the Sachar Committee has demonstrated. Although his Government had announced several welfare schemes, the fact poverty levels of the Dalits and Adivasis, as we have shown, persist and do not show any tangible evidence of progress in their lives; one wonders who these people are who are being benefitted from these programmes. Mr Modi is effective in using the Hindu religion card to bash Muslims, Christians, and -Pakistan as a sponsor of terrorists to gain the Hindu vote. Although most Hindus are tolerant people, showing no prejudice towards Muslims, There is a section of people who show a visceral reaction in mentioning the name Muslims and Pakistan, perhaps due to the long-running conflict India has with Pakistan over the Kashmir issue. Mr Modi enjoys support among caste Hindus, especially from the other backward class people who have joined the middle-class status (he enjoys a 57% approval rating). As we have mentioned, currently, 800 million Indians are living in poverty, getting some rations for free from the Government, while the number of billionaires has been increasing in India on Modi's watch. For example, according to Forbes India magazine (October 16, 2023), the number of Indian billionaires stood at 169 for 2023. The Modi regime has adopted centralised capitalism by giving Government contracts and subsidies to a few handfuls of millionaires and billionaires. It is called crony capitalism. This is why there is economic stagnation (around 6.3 %), with growing unemployment among the youth remaining at 20%. Decentralisation of the economy is imperative if India must grow to grow economically at a rapid rate. India is the most unequal country in the world. The top 10% and 1% hold 57% and 22% of the total national income, respectively, while the bottom 50% share has gone down to 13%. The average national income is Rs 2,02200, while the bottom 50% earns Rs. 53,610, and the top 10% earns Rs 11 66 520 (*The Economic Times*, Dec 21, 2021). These figures denote that the Government's economic policies may have to be evaluated on how to narrow such a huge disparity between the rich and the poor. Many Indians are renouncing their Indian citizenship and leaving the country. For example, according to the External Ministry, in 2022, 2,25,620 had renounced their citizenship, and the number stands at 17.5 lakhs from 2011 to the present (*The Economic Times*, July 23, 2023). This figure denotes a loss of the brain drain. Most of the best and the brightest, the cream of India, who graduate from IITSs, go to the west, especially the US. Many of them may not leave the country if proper incentives are provided. If they do stay, they can play a significant role in India's development as the best and the brightest Chinese have stayed back in the country and have contributed mightily to the rapid industrialisation of China and making it become a superpower.

India needs secular and class-based parties, all-encompassing all ethnic and religious groups, not communal or caste-based and family-based, to make India a fully integrated, unified, and caste-less egalitarian country. This is possible if Indians choose secular leaders who respect all people and all religions with equanimity and commitment to the common good of all people. The leaders and demagogues who appeal to certain people's prejudices, bigotry, and fears and find escape gates in other groups for the country's problems to gain power and then undermine democratic institutions should never be allowed to gain political power. A few months ago, more than 26 political parties had formed a coalition called India. It remains to be seen whether they give up their sectional interests and transcend them to challenge the BJP as a cohesive and united party with a promise of a minimum policy agenda and restoration of secularism. If they do, they could win in the upcoming May 2024 elections, and restore India's secular credentials and work for the common good of all Indians. Secularism does not oppose religion. It only calls for the separation of church and state. As the US example indicates, religion flourishes when there is separation between church and state, and the church almost dies, as is the case in Western Europe, where church and state are merged. Unfortunately, some Indian politicians are too ambitious and power-hungry to transcend their regional fiefdoms and work as patriotic Indians to redeem India of hate and sectarian nationalism. The US Freedom House and the Economist have ranked India under Modi as "partially free." Perhaps Modi was the first Prime Minister who never wanted to hold a press conference to explain or defend his policies despite the fact that he had put major portions of India's press/media under his thumb. What explains his reluctance is hard to decipher. Is it his sense of insecurity or sense of inadequacy to answer questions or contempt for the press? We do not know.

Let us look at what is happening in Manipur, where violence has gripped the state since May 3, 2023, between the Meitei- the Hindu majority community and the Kuki – Christian Minority Community. The Manipur state High Court's granting of backward class status to Meiteis was the primary cause that triggered the civil strife between these communities. As of mid-September, 200 people have been killed, leaving more than 70,000 displaced, who are mostly Kukis. The violence resulted in extensive damage to religious institutions, mostly churches and left the people with digital lockouts and overcrowded relief camps without an effective f Government response led by inept Chief Minister Biren Singh of the BJP. While violence was raging in the state, Mr. Modi had never said a word about the Manipur crisis until late in July when two raped, naked Kuki women were paraded on TV. It was only then that Mr. Modi made a statement in parliament, denouncing the incident and committing his Government to develop the state. He never visited the state despite several pleas from people from

Manipur and opposition leaders. Only his Home Minister, Mr. Amit Shaah visited the state. It is hard to figure out why Mr Modi does not want to visit the state. However, his tepid repose and lack of interest in the crisis denotes, perhaps, his lack of interest in the crisis as Prime Minister of the country.[59]

India-Canadian relations have reached a low point over the assassination of Hardeep Singh Vijjar, a Canadian citizen and Sikh separatist leader in Vancouver, B.C, in June 2023 near the Gurdwara., whom India considered a "terrorist." Apparently, on a credible report provided by his intelligence agencies that Indian agents were involved in Mr Vijjar's killing, Prime Minister Justin Trudeau asked Mr Modi for his cooperation in the investigation when the latter met Mr Modi during the August G-20 held in Delhi. Subsequently, Mr Trudeau openly implicated Delhi in the killing and sought its cooperation, which angered India. India denied its involvement and called the allegation "absurd" However, supported by the five- -country intelligence- US, UK, Australia, NJ, and Canada known as "five-eyes," Canada stands by its accusation, which has resulted in an escalation of tensions between the two countries. India has demanded that Canada withdraw its overstaffed diplomats on a parity basis with Indian diplomats in Canada, to which the latter has withdrawn 42 diplomats from India in late October. The Canadian For the suspension of visa, consular services at the consulate in Chandigarh, Mumbai, and Bangalore, and indicating that the visa services will be available only at the Canadian High Commission in Delhi.[60] About 1.6 million Indians live in Canada, excluding more than 700,000 Sikhs, some of whom are active in Canadian politics. Some of them are serving in Trudeau's cabinet. Sikhs were the first people who migrated to Canada as members of the Gadder party, escaping the British arrest and persecution in India. However, most of them do not support Khalistan. About 200,000 Indian students are attending Canadian universities and colleges. Among the Western countries, Canada has been the most welcoming country to Indians and others to emigrate. Now that tensions have broken out with Canada, the Canadian Consulate services have been

---

[59] For more details on Manipur crisis, see Ali, "The Manipur Crisis: Four months of Unending Violence", Genocide Watch, September 14, 2023, at https://www.genocidewatch.com/single-post/the-manipur-crisis--four-months of-unending-violence.

[60] "Canada halts Visa Consular services in Chandigarh, Mubai, Banglore Consulates", Deccan Chronicle, October 20, 2023, at https://www//deccanchronicle.com/world/europe/201023/canada-suspends-visa-and-consular-services-at-three-consulates.html.

suspended. Indians may find it hard to get their applications processed to emigrate to Canada. This way, India is a loser in this diplomatic tussle. Incidentally, if the opposition is not careful in commenting on the current tensions with Canada, Mr Modi may use this issue to bash the opposition and Canada to zin up the support for his party in the upcoming May 2024 elections.

Hinduism conceives "the world as a family" (Vasudha Iva Kutumba am), a noble idea. If that is the belief, it should start at home, transcending all religions and castes, caring for one another and threatening others as equals by getting rid of the abhorrent practice of the caste system and untouchability and treating Muslims and Dalits as equal partners in building and transforming India into an egalitarian prosperous country. It is only then Indi can command respect at home and abroad as an exemplary democracy worthy to emulate. India needs to develop a degree of homogeneity for Indians to think of themselves as Indians first and last, not defining themselves as Andras Tamils, Punjabis, Maharashtrians, etc., so essential to build a sense of community and oneness,

Ambedkar as its own, not because it believes in any of his principles, but because to get a Dalit vote in the name of Ambedkar, revered by all Dalits. It is ironic that Modi claims India to be Vishwa Guru. The atrocities being committed against Dalits and Adivasis are comparable to what Whites in the US South used to commit even after blacks had gained the right of citizenship and civil rights under amendments 13, 14, and 15 in 1865, 1866 and 1968, respectively, following the end of civil war (1861-65). Yet southern states had committed many egregious atrocities, including lynchings, commonly known as Jim Crow laws against blacks. It was only after approval of the Civil Rights Act of 1964 and the Voting Rights Act of 1965 under the presidency of Lyndon Johnson (1963-69) that the South civil and voting rights of blacks were restored, and that enabled Barak Obama, a black person to get elected President in 2008.

Conclusion

We conclude that Hinduism is a religion which is caste-based, hierarchical, unequal, discriminatory, and even violent towards minorities such as Muslims and Dalits. The caste system is entrenched, and it is so deep caste

Hindus may not find it extremely difficult to purge themselves of their sense of superiority and purity and accept Dalits and Adivasis as their equals as human beings entitled to dignity and respect as they are. Upper-caste Hindus are socialised from their childhood into believing that they are distinguished and culturally and even racially superior, although some of the Dalits and Adivasis look much light-skinned than the so-called Aryans, as we have mentioned. The atrocities and attacks on the Dalits have increased under the Modi regime, although he is himself a Shudra. Unlike other major religions, Hinduism is pantheistic, with about 33-330 million gods and goddesses. It is the blatant discrimination and oppression by upper castes with impunity and with no accountability that has caused the Dalits to live in perpetual poverty and socio-economic deprivation. Untouchability is a heinous practice. Yet, it still continues in India unabated, even in this highly rational and technological 21st century. In the next chapter, we want to briefly discuss the beliefs about men and women, slavery, their practices, and their impact on India's caste system.